A FRIENDLY ALLIANCE

HEIRS OF BERKSHIRE BOOK ONE

KAREN LYNNE

A Friendly Alliance

Heirs of Berkshire Book One

Copyright © 2020 by Karen Evelyn.

Rev. 2

OTHER BOOKS BY KAREN LYNNE

Brides of Somerset Series

Heirs of Berkshire Series

Join my reader's group and enjoy updates for new books and little bits of tidbits on 19th-century history.

Juliana Gibbon picked her way through the oak trees, lifting her skirts as she moved through the thick brush, stepping carefully to keep from dragging her hem in the mud as she headed toward *her lake*. The lake bordered her father's property a mile from the house. It was situated down a slight hill surrounded by oaks, some of them gnarled, giving them a gothic look. She often slipped away from her nanny to relax by its bank, always making the trek on foot. The peace it offered rivaled nothing she'd yet to experience. Her place of solitude, she'd visited it often over the thirteen years she'd been on this earth. She'd filled her pockets with seeds and breadcrumbs to feed the ducks that paddled on the lake, which she did often and not a soul minded. Well, perhaps one minded, but he was preparing to leave for Cambridge in a few days.

She tried not to think about the fact that all her friends had a governess long before her. Her father's failure in hiring one was being remedied this very day, thanks to Lady Berkshire. She knew her father loved her but still thought her a child.

As she reached the slope leading to the lake, she heard water splashing. Ducking behind a tree, she peered around its trunk, fixing her blue eyes on the water. Peter Seton, the Earl of Berkshire's son, glided effortlessly, his long arms slicing through the water.

Her bottom lip curled downward. She wouldn't be able to feed the ducks. He was wasting her morning. This lake was *hers*. Truly, he shouldn't even be here. Rumors of him preparing for school had been flying about the house all week. Pressing forward, she moved closer down the slope to get a better look.

She watched him easily perform backstrokes, his arms keeping him afloat with each stroke. The trees' shade cast dappled light on his relaxed features, and she envied his peaceful escape.

Juliana froze as she noticed what he wore, or was *not* wearing. Peter was in his underclothes. A pile of his cast-off clothing sat on the bank. She knew she shouldn't but curiosity kept her moving closer to get a better look. Peter never took her seriously. It was time to teach him a lesson.

She and her father had frequented Alder Court

because they were neighbors. Peter and she had played together. He was like the brother she never had.

She stopped, steadying herself on a small tree.

Peter was five years her senior, but spying on him now, he looked almost a full-grown man. She pushed that thought to the back of her mind and realized she was intruding. How very inappropriate to see a half-dressed gentleman, even if it was just Peter.

Juliana stepped back, retracing her steps, backtracking home. If caught spying on him, she'd get a tongue lashing from her nanny or her father or worse.

The new governess.

As she moved around the tree, her foot moved on the slick mud, and down she went, grasping at the trunk. A cry slipped out. Holding on tight, she turned her head toward the lake, hoping she hadn't been heard.

"Who's there?" Peter's voice rang out.

He swam closer to the bank and stood, blinking water from his eyes.

"Juliana?" He paused, wiping the water from his face.

Mortification heated her cheeks as she took in his naked chest.

He blinked again, as if she were an apparition.

"Juliana, were you—spying on me?" His hands went to his hips in indignation.

"No!" she found her voice. "I was coming to feed the ducks."

Peter waded out of the water and reached for his shirt, pulling it over his head with purposeful movements. She should have felt some embarrassment but found she was too afraid he would tell her father and he would ban her from visiting the lake. Her days would become a drudgery of lessons and etiquette.

"It's highly unconventional for a young lady to spy on a gentleman, and in his underclothes no less." His honey-colored curls hung dark and limp from the water, causing his locks to look much straighter, no longer curling about his neck.

Juliana crossed her arms. "I wasn't spying," she argued, her brows drawn.

Peter dried his hair with a thin towel, his curls bouncing back to where they belonged.

"You understand that this lake belongs to me?"

"It does not, Peter Seton! This lake has been in my family for ages. I can show you the papers to prove it!" She had never actually seen the papers, but she'd overheard her father talking to his solicitor about it once. "Besides, no one loves it the way I do. I've been tending it my entire life!"

"A lake does not need tending." Peter retorted, a smile replacing his anger.

She stood taller, relieved Peter was no longer irritated with her.

"It does too! I've cleared a spot by its bank every spring so I could feed the ducks."

"Well, I've been swimming in it since before you were born. The lake belongs to me."

"You are only five years my senior. I highly doubt that!" She laughed, glad they had restored their friendly banter.

He let out a chuckle, and she tried not to smile. He was winning this argument merely because they allowed him to be here, and she was not. His claim was stronger by the fact of his gender… and he was the earl's only son.

"I *may* allow you to swim in it if you let me join you in a hunt this season." She waited for his scolding, but he laughed instead, waving his hand at her dismissively.

"Run home to your nanny."

Juliana stood to her full height, lifting her chin. "I have a governess now. She comes this very day."

Peter had finished dressing. His loose white shirt and gray trousers gave him a casual air. He held his waistcoat over his arm as he stepped toward her, edging his way up the hill.

"Moving up in the world I see," his brown eyes laughing at her.

He stood a full foot taller, but she remained where she was on the slope so she could match his height. Refusing to show he affected her with his teasing. No one knew she had a secret crush on him.

"Yes, but you have not answered my request to join the hunt."

Peter leaned his arm against a trunk and cocked a brow. "You would fall off your horse."

"How can you say that? I ride as well as your friends."

"That may be, let's see… I'll let you join the hunt when you can hit three targets in a row with your bow and arrow." He smiled, goading her further. "I seem to remember you struggling to draw the bow at my mother's last picnic."

Juliana frowned. "So you think if I can hit the targets with my arrows, I will be able to stay on my horse?"

"We'll see," he said.

She so desperately wanted to master the bow but struggled to draw the string, let alone hitting the target. The fact he was using it against her caused her temper to flare.

"Then you must teach me," she spouted.

"I think not, I am much too busy," he paused, a slow, mischievous smile lighting his face, "—away hunting." He pushed off the tree trunk and backed away from her.

She stomped her foot. "Then how am I to learn?" She knew he was baiting her on purpose, but she couldn't stop herself. He had intruded on her solitude and now was mocking her all because she was a girl.

Peter tousled her hair before retreating down the slope. He turned back, giving her that smile. "If you practice while I am away and can hit three targets with your arrow, then when I return, I'll let you join the hunt."

She stumbled down the slope, catching up to him. "Where are you going?"

"I'm leaving for Cambridge this week."

He had confirmed her suspicions. He was leaving, and she was losing her friend. She'd resisted the impulse to think of him as a man, but the undeniable proof stood before her. He was leaving her behind. Not just for university, but leaving their childhood behind as well.

He nodded with a smile. "My mother wants me to begin acting like a respectable young man."

"But you just returned from school." She willed him to reassure her that things would be as they were before.

"Yes, and now that I have passed my exams, I must become acquainted with my place in society." He winked at her before turning away, heading back toward Alder Court.

She watched him move out of sight. Something inside turned hollow as he disappeared from view. Juliana turned up the slope, forced to return home to her father where her new governess awaited. Her playmate from youth had turned into a man in front of her eyes, ready to become stuffy and old. Though Peter would probably call it distinguished.

She giggled at the thought.

CHAPTER 1

FIVE YEARS LATER...

Juliana tucked a piece of toast drizzled with honey into her mouth and licked her fingers. She lifted her eyes to find Miss Stringham, her governess, shaking her head slightly. Juliana lowered her hand and slid the napkin to her lap, wiping her wet fingers dry. Her father sifted through the morning mail across from her, oblivious to her slip in etiquette. Their days had slipped into a daily routine these past five years. She didn't mind so much aside from the fact that she yearned for adventure, which Miss Stringham tried to supply as best she could while teaching her to be a lady.

"Have I told you your aunt and uncle are coming next week to take you to London?" her father grumbled.

"Many times papa. I am grateful to them—and you, of course, for letting me go." She smiled inwardly at his attempts to bring up the touchy subject. *Despite the delay.*

He huffed, tossing a few letters onto the table. "I still think you should wait until next year. Or better yet, don't go at all."

"You've insisted I wait until *this* year already. And if I don't go, how am I ever to find a husband?" Juliana forced a smile. They'd been over this many times in the last few weeks. Her father had thrown excuses at her to keep her by his side. "You're afraid I'll get swept up by a man with no prospects or money, aren't you?" she teased.

Her father had encouraged Juliana's independent mind, gave her a warm place to grow with lots of love far removed from society as it was. She loved having Miss Stringham, who taught her the refined arts of a lady. It was time he allowed her to put that training to work.

He grunted, refusing to look at her. "You would do very well to remain here by my side."

"Lady Berkshire and Miss Stringham have explained that it is every young lady's privilege to have a season at least once. How else may I meet the right gentleman?"

"I see no reason you can't find him here. I will give you a ball and invite all the eligible boys in the county."

Juliana snorted before composing herself. "You

dislike balls. I might as well marry Peter so you would not have to bother making yourself uncomfortable."

His eyes widened with a smile. "That is a capital idea. I shall go to Alder Court and talk to the Earl as soon as breakfast is over. Of course, my sister-in-law will be disappointed."

Juliana stood abruptly. "You will do no such thing. Peter is like a brother to me. I would rather become an old maid before becoming *his* wife! What would Lady Berkshire think?"

"You do the Setons a disservice. Any intelligent young lady would jump at the chance of catching a future earl. You couldn't do better than Peter Seton."

Juliana's face heated. She hadn't seen Peter since he left for Cambridge. She could think of a thousand reasons they would not suit. He would scold her at every turn. She would have more freedom remaining in her father's house. Her entire life, she'd followed him around trying to have him teach her things girls weren't allowed to do. Only to be put off with jests or ultimatums. She remembered his last challenge. Peter leaning an arm against the tree trunk, his cocked brow mocking her.

"I'll let you join the hunt when you can hit three targets in a row with your bow and arrow." He smiled, goading her. *"I seem to remember you struggling to draw the bow at my mother's last picnic."*

She had practiced her archery. Her father even

bought her a bow she could pull. If she ever had the chance, she would show Peter.

"Well Juliana, if you are against the match, I won't trouble myself on a useless errand." Her father turned his attention back to the mail, opening the last piece and scanning its contents, bringing the subject to a close.

She thought.

"Lord Berkshire's hunting party is tomorrow." He paused, his eyes moving over the paper again. "I've been invited."

Juliana dropped back into her seat, no longer disturbed by her father's threats of marriage. Lord Berkshire would have laughed.

"Will you go?" She leaned on the table, reaching for the invitation.

He shook his head, lifting the card out of her reach. "No. No, I don't think I will. I'm getting too old for these things, you know." His eyes twinkled. Father knew her obsession with the hunt. He was teasing her about her marriage prospects… and the hunt. Sometimes she wished her mother was still alive. Like Peter, he had been obstinate in his resolve at refusing her this pleasure.

Juliana coaxed her voice into a sweet tone. "May I go in your stead, please, papa? Miss Stringham will accompany me."

"For the hunt? With the men? I don't think so, Juliana." He shook his head. "Best stay here. It is too dangerous for a girl to be chasing a fox about the countryside."

Juliana's jaw clenched. Miss Stringham watched as she struggled to regain her composure.

"Mr. Gibbon, Juliana is a capable horsewoman. Other ladies will take part, so she will not be alone," Miss Stringham reassured him.

"Lord Berkshire will look after me. Please?" Juliana didn't dare breathe.

He turned, the worried expression in his aging eyes had eased at Miss Stringham's urging. He was thinking. Juliana didn't like it when he thought. She could tell by his demeanor. It would not end well. If he allowed her to ride in the hunt, would he stop her from going to London for a season hoping for a match with Peter?

"I've been practicing with the bow you gave me." Her father had been impressed with her improvement. She pressed him further. "Peter has promised to let me join the hunt if I hit the targets with my arrow."

Her father rubbed the side of his face. "It would do Peter good to see your improvement and the lady you've become, thanks to Miss Stringham. It may intrigue him to see your skill." He turned toward her.

She smiled affectionately. "I shall do you proud. Please say yes."

"I suppose if Peter will look after you and make sure you stay out of trouble."

Juliana held in her exasperation. "Papa, I'm capable of keeping *myself* out of trouble if I so choose."

"Quite right," he said, cutting into his pastry and taking a bite. "Yes," he paused. "you may go if Miss Stringham accompanies you."

Juliana's smile stretched. "Thank you!"

He smiled affectionately before dabbing his napkin to his mustache, then laying it on the table. He stood, moving to his study, leaving her alone to form her plan. Papa was the first hurdle. Peter was the second. Would he keep his word if she hit the targets? She wasn't sure who was more stubborn, her father or Peter.

She knew spending a season in London would be hard for her father. Ever since her mother had died giving birth to her sister, both of them lying in a grave, she had become his life. She should have gone two seasons ago when she turned seventeen, now she would turn nineteen while in London. Her friend Silvia had been to London every year since she could walk and had boasted about the fact every chance she got. Silvia's father was a member of parliament, she knew the city well.

Benham Park had always been Juliana's home. She had never left Newbury, though it was just a stone's throw from London. Her father preferred the country and saw no reason to leave.

She stood. "Miss Stringham, I would like to practice

my archery this morning. I want to be ready for the hunting party."

Miss Stringham smiled and set down her tea. "I'll be in the library when you're ready to pick your dress for the party."

Leaving the breakfast room alone, Juliana checked on her father. Once she knew he was comfortable, she hurried to change and gather her equipment. Once outside she walked to Alder Court determined to show Peter her skills. She strolled onto the lawn and toward the stables, hoping he had returned from his morning ride, her bow strung across her shoulder.

John, the head stable hand, brushed Beast, Peter's stallion, his eyes seeking hers when she entered the stable yard.

"Good morning, Miss Juliana. You heard Master Peter was home?" His smile grew as she stepped closer.

John had been a servant for the Setons since she could remember. His youthful hair held a touch of grey, making him appear older than he was.

"Yes." She smiled, patting Beast's muzzle, wishing she'd brought a treat.

"Master Peter hasn't left yet. I expect him shortly." The groom finished cinching the saddle strap.

The crunch of gravel sounded, and Juliana turned. Peter strode toward her, his eyebrows raised, studying her intently. Her heart stuttered while catching her breath. Could Peter have changed so much in five years?

His black riding jacket fit to perfection over a bright green waistcoat. A broad chest and shapely legs replaced his boyish figure without an ounce of extra fat. She wished she had taken better care of her dress. She should have worn one of the new ones. She lifted her hand to check her hair. At least she had worn a bonnet.

"Is this Juliana, the young girl I left behind five years back?" He circled, making her feel shy.

He reached out, took her hand and, raising it to his lips, brushed a kiss across her knuckles, smiling. "You've grown up."

"As have you. Hesitation hung as she bit at her bottom lip.

She extracted her hand, rubbing it across her skirt.

He laughed, a deep sound that had her heart pumping again. "Touché"

He fingered her bow and sheaf of arrows. "You heard about tomorrow's hunting party."

"I have. And I've come to hit the targets and join the party."

He grinned and looked at John. "I will not be riding Beast this morning. Have Jacob take him out to give him his head. I want him ready for the hunting party tomorrow." He turned back to Juliana, his smile growing. "You really think you are ready for a hunt?" His tone condescending as he teased her.

She smacked his arm, but he tugged her hand into his with a laugh. "By all means, test your skills." He didn't let go of her hand as he pulled her to the archery range behind the stables.

Juliana let him guide her, gently removing her hand from his grasp as she stood before the targets. Squaring her shoulders, she stepped to the women's line. Taking a deep breath, she drew a shaft from the quiver and placed it against the string. She turned to the side, ignoring Peter standing behind her. She eyed the bullseye on the first target, pulled back with even pressure, aimed, and released the arrow. It sailed straight and sure.

With a quick *thwack,* the arrow lodged on the edge of the bullseye. *Still counts,* she thought before removing another arrow and aiming at the second target. She focused, willing her aim to be true. It hit the center of the target, and she smiled smugly to herself. Her practice was paying off.

Peter didn't make a sound, only watched.

She faced the third and final target, confident she would hit the bullseye. Releasing the third arrow, her heart plummeted in dismay as it hit just outside the bullseye. She pressed her lips together and spun to face Peter.

He clapped slowly. "Well done. Too bad about that last one. I will miss you on the hunt tomorrow." His last word held a teasing note.

"As I recall, when the *Honorable* Peter Seton made

our deal several years ago, he said I could attend the hunt if I could *hit* three targets. You never specified where." She smiled.

"It was implied," he said dryly.

Frustration bubbled in her chest. "I am leaving next week to prepare for my first season. Who knows? I may find an eligible suitor. This may be my only chance to hunt with your party again."

Peter took several steps toward her, stopping by her side. "Perhaps if you improve, this new suitor will let you join him in his own hunting party—May I?"

She didn't resist when he took her bow from her hands and fitted an arrow. In quick succession, he hit the bullseye of each target. He turned to her with a grin, his eyes sparkling with mirth.

Juliana shook her head. "All right, I will admit I am not as good as you *yet,* but I am better than average." She plucked her bow back from him. "Admit it, I have proved myself a capable shot."

"You have," Peter admitted, his teasing gone, overshadowed with concern. "But will you be able to stay in your seat? It can be quite rigorous when the hounds catch the scent of the fox. I worry what your father would think of you riding across the fields."

"He has given me his blessing if Miss Stringham comes with me."

"Miss Stringham?"

"My governess."

Peter laughed, catching her cheek in a small pinch. "I suppose if your father approves, who am I to say no." He bowed, taking Juliana's hand. "Miss Gibbon, would you do me the honor of joining our hunting party tomorrow?" His familiar eyes sparkled.

She nearly squealed with excitement, then remembered what Miss Stringham had taught her. She lifted her head, eyes peering at Peter. "I would," she replied, giving him her best curtsy.

CHAPTER 2

SARAH, Juliana's maid, tucked in the last curl, pinning her hat in place. "You look lovely, Miss Juliana."

Juliana stepped back, admiring her profile in the mirror. The color of her new riding habit set off her complexion, and the cut enhanced her figure. She was no longer a child and determined to prove it.

Miss Stringham joined her as they rode to Alder Court. Her governess was as proficient in the saddle as she, giving her the confidence she needed. She'd waited so long to be a part of the hunt the Setons hosted annually. It was a grand affair, bringing half the neighbors together after the harvest was in. She had been attending the house party since she was a child and was fascinated with the red coats and baying hounds. Today she would be part of it.

The gentlemen had gathered on the edge of the

field. She could feel the excitement of the hounds as they bayed underfoot, running between the horses' legs, nipping and howling, waiting to be off. Most of the gentlemen she knew from the gatherings over the years, but the Earl of Berkshire performed the duty of hunt master along with several neighbors as joint masters.

She led her mare amongst the gentlemen, heading toward Peter, who sat atop Beast, talking with his father.

Lord Berkshire tilted his head. "Good day, Miss Gibbon. A pleasure to see you as always. Peter tells me you will be joining the chase." His smile stretched, underlying his formal address to her.

"Yes, my lord." She glanced around the group. "I feel the thrill already!"

Gentlemen eyed her with curiosity. A handful of women were joining them. His hunt was notorious for its masculine presence which was exactly why she'd been so obsessed with it, though she'd never admit it to Peter.

Mr. Hampton called to her from atop his black stallion, his ruddy face peeled open with a grin. "Joining us today, Miss Gibbon?"

"I am," she said proudly. "By the invitation of the honorable Peter Seton."

"Upon my word!" Mr. Norman broke into her conversation. Tall, proud, and newly married and also quite vocal about wanting to have his pleasures without the women intruding. "You must keep up and retain your seat. We shall not give way if you cannot keep up."

"Have no fear on my behalf, sir. Lord Berkshire himself can attest to my abilities"

Mr. Norman married a soft-spoken, dull, but practical wife who didn't mind sitting by the side. Juliana, never shy, wanted to be in the fray of it all.

Lord Berkshire laughed. "There is plenty of sport to be had by all!" He gave Juliana a wink, and she smiled in fondness and delight. She should have made her appeal to him in the first place.

As the trumpet sounded, the gentlemen and ladies set off through the woods, following the hounds baying at the signal and coming alive with the chase.

Before she could prompt her own horse to follow, Mr. Hampton engaged her in conversation. "The weather has been kind today, allowing for an unusually fine hunt. I am sure the fox will give a good chase."

Juliana couldn't believe this man was talking of the weather. Of all the things to stop her, Mr. Hampton's light conversation was not one she would have expected. She quickly lost patience at being left behind.

"Shall we join the chase?" she spurred her mare forward.

Peter soon lost sight of Juliana as he moved to follow the hounds through the trees. He understood why Juliana wanted to take part. Sometimes the fox was caught, sometimes not, but that didn't matter. It was the sport that thrilled him.

When he first set eyes on Juliana at the stables, he was shocked, surprised, delighted as all the emotions ran together. Gone was the skinny girl with flowing locks and in her place a woman of substance. Can a person change in five short years? She had grown up, to be sure. A light sprinkling of freckles still dotted her nose, a testament she still went without her bonnet, but she'd filled out in all the right places. He chuckled to himself. She'd remembered his silly challenge.

A commotion ahead brought his attention back to the party. Men quickly approached, shouting for him to come.

His senses pricked at the distress in Mr. Norman's urgent words. "Peter, come quickly, your father has fallen!"

His heart plummeted as Mr. Norman's words took root. He turned his horse and sped toward his father, pushing away uneasy thoughts. Pulling the reins tightly, he stopped just before the gathered group. In one fluid motion, he dismounted and fell to the ground near his father's lifeless body.

"What has happened?" His urgency grew tenfold as he noticed blood pooling under his father's body, too much blood. He pulled his riding coat off and ripped his shirtsleeve clean off, tying the white cloth around his father's head, but blood still seeped through the cloth.

"No one knows. It happened so quickly. One moment he was atop his horse shouting commands to the hounds, and the next he was falling to the ground."

"There is too much blood." Peter fingered his father's head looking for the wound. He didn't wait for a reply, shouting his next command. Fear ripped through him. "Fetch the doctor."

A servant beside him responded, "Alister already went for him Master Peter."

"There was too much commotion—I," Mr. Hampton stammered. "The horse stumbled, and he fell."

Peter tried to calm his trembling hands, no one was to blame, but the panic didn't leave his chest. His father had not responded to Peter's errant hands shaking him to wake. His chest did not fall... Peter closed his eyes tightly as he willed this nightmare away.

Silence settled on the group as they waited for the doctor to confirm their suspicions. His father was dead, a gash to the head, and no one could bring him back. The doctor pronounced Lord Berkshire deceased, and Peter's spirits dropped fully. A thousand thoughts raced through his mind as the surrounding noise echoed in his brain.

Mr. Norman's voice broke through the fog, bringing

him back to the present. "You might want the doctor to look you over. You've paled considerably."

Peter shook his head. "Return without me." Jumping on his mount, he galloped away. He needed to think. He needed to breathe.

Reaching the edge of the lake, he dismounted and walked to the water. He stared at its calm, peaceful appearance. Picking up a stone, he violently chucked it into the lake, watching the water ripple as it plunged underneath.

"Peter?" Juliana's voice cut through his torment.

He startled as he noticed her eyes held a slight sheen. She'd been crying. Did she already know? "Juliana, what are you doing out here?" His voice cracked, and he watched her sadness turn to concern.

Her blue eyes locked on his, concern showed on her face. Juliana inched closer, her eyes soft and warm. Peter didn't want to say the words out loud, as if speaking would complete this nightmare. He looked out at the lake, which had resumed its peaceful reverie. "My father—" he broke, unable to finish his sentence. He shook his head, crossing his arms and struggling to control his emotion.

"I'm sorry," she whispered.

"He's dead," Peter blurted.

Juliana set a light hand on his arm. Despite the heat of the day, Peter felt cold. He turned, taking in her distressed expression.

"I know—" She cleared the frog from her throat, squeezing her eyes tightly closed. She was trying to keep it together. He reached for her before thinking better of it. He pulled his hand back.

"What happened?" she finally asked, her voice steadier as tears ran down her cheek despite her closed eyes.

"He fell from his horse," he choked out, bile rising in his throat.

A cry escaped her lips as her eyes flew open. He pulled her to him, letting her tears dampen his shirt. He twisted his fingers through her loose hair, holding her to him, gaining strength, and comforting her at the same time.

A silence settled between them as her tears dried. "Would you like to be alone?" She tilted her head slightly, matching his eyes. He slipped his fingers down, catching the back of her neck. She snatched his hand and slid it to her lips, placing a quick kiss upon it before dropping his hand and taking a slow step out of his embrace.

Peter focused on Juliana's features, ignoring her disheveled hair, her hat thoughtlessly tossed aside. Sometimes he still viewed her as a little girl, but in this moment, in the wake of his father's death, he realized she had grown into a fine young woman.

He looked away. "I just need to absorb the information."

"If there is even the smallest comfort, I can offer you–" Juliana started.

"I can imagine very little comfort at this moment." He tightened his fists. "Forgive me. Perhaps it is best I am left alone for now."

She watched him silently for a few moments before stepping away from his side. "We'll be awaiting your return at Alder Court."

He closed his eyes and listened as Juliana mounted her mare and rode away, leaving him alone in his grief.

CHAPTER 3

THE CLOUDS SAT heavy the day they buried the late Lord Berkshire. It had been a week since Juliana had seen the family. She stood with her father amongst friends and acquaintances as the parish priest read words she did not wish to hear. They encircled Lord Berkshire's gravesite. The hole not yet filled. She'd formed a close attachment to Peter's father. Though he'd been a solitary man who liked to keep to himself—the complete opposite of his wife—she'd woven her way into his heart. Juliana watched Lady Berkshire, sobbing quietly into her handkerchief as she clutched Peter like a lifeline, her face twisted in a mournful grimace.

Sorrow tugged at Juliana as she glanced at the pair. Peter stood resolute, emotionless, like a statue. He was now the Earl. At just twenty and three, he seemed too young for the momentous task of running the estate.

Juliana's father stood soberly next to her. Lord Berkshire was his friend and Juliana feared he would take his passing hard, just as he had her mother's.

The service drew to a close. Peter and their now surviving parents moved away from the gravesite. Peter's head hung, his mother grasping his arm for support as silent sobs heaved his shoulders. Juliana placed her foot forward ready to offer comfort but was stopped by a sob of sorrow beside her. She moved to her father, propping him up. She needed to be his stalwart buoy now. Peter had his mother for comfort. With a jerk of her heart, she led her father to their coach, giving them one last chance to be alone as a family.

Friends, neighbors and tenants stopped at Alder Court to pay their respects, talking in low tones about the significant loss of the Earl. Lady Berkshire had insisted on providing a meal, which had been set up on the grounds. The gathering went quiet when Peter and Lady Berkshire arrived from the graveside. Lady Berkshire's eyes glistened with unshed tears as she spoke quietly to Peter, then retreated into her home.

"Lady Berkshire wishes to thank you for your attendance today in honor of my father. I know you'll understand her wish to retire," Peter announced.

Juliana listened while she sat next to her father in the shade of the trees, Miss Stringham on his other side. Peter mingled with those wishing him condolences. She felt out of place and useless as she watched Peter taking over in his father's stead. This was real, she hadn't dreamed it.

Peter's emotionless eyes lit with relief at the sight of her beside him. "Juliana—thank you for coming."

She bit her bottom lip, trying to stifle her grief at his quiet whisper.

"Of course." She gulped at her lame response, but what could she say that would make it bearable?

Peter swirled the glass in his hand. "I know you were looking forward to visiting your uncle. I am sorry I'm making you delayed."

Her heart leaped, squeezing her chest. Did he think she would abandon him at this agonizing moment? "Do not apologize. I would rather be with you in your time of need." Placing a hand on his forearm, she offered him a smile, one that he returned with a slight curl of his lips.

"Truly, how are you doing?" she whispered, tilting her head close to his. Her body tingled at their closeness.

"I haven't slept," he admitted. "I want nothing more than to mount Beast and ride until I reach the sea and then scream my misfortunes."

Juliana laughed softly. "I'm afraid you would have a long ride, and the sea would not understand you."

"No," he sighed. "But I'd have it off my chest." He paused, swallowing. "It happened so suddenly I didn't get the chance to say goodbye."

Juliana squeezed his arm before a couple she didn't recognize came to Peter, offering their condolences. She made to leave, when Peter's hand caught her fingers behind his back, tightening as if to say, *Stay a moment.* She stilled, and stood just behind his left shoulder as he answered each guest with responses, his fingers entwined with hers, refusing to let go. A break in the crowd had him relaxed just a moment.

"Thank you," he murmured. "Your presence gives me the strength I need."

"Of course," Juliana sighed.

She was glad to be of service, anything. So she stood rooted to his side while he faced the fellow mourners. Peter did not release her, but stood straighter. She stayed firm even as reproachful glances flew her way. She would not feel regret next to Peter. He had helped her through many less trying scrapes over the years. And now he needed her, so she'd stand here as long as he wished. They were childhood friends, after all.

Peter would not be coming to London for this year's season. She listened as Peter explained his altered plans. Disappointment curled in her breast, but she brushed it away. Her purpose in going to London was to become acquainted with others in society and to find a husband. Their closeness could very well chase away potential suitors.

It was for the best, she tried to reassure herself.

The afternoon deepened, and guests slipped away. Juliana moved from Peter's side, slipping into the great hall, and moved quietly to the drawing room where Lady Berkshire sat in her favorite chair. Lord Berkshire's chair sat opposite. The fire had dimmed, and no one had bothered to stir it back to life. Juliana's heart constricted seeing this lively woman looking so lost. She kneeled at Lady Berkshire's side, taking the limp hand in hers. Lady Berkshire's white face and hollow eyes came to life at the touch.

"Juliana dear, are you still here? Your father, is he well?" The woman sat up, rearranging her countenance as if to shake away her sorrow.

"Don't worry. My father is well. I just wanted to say my goodbyes before I left. I am not sure if I shall have time to see you before I leave for London." Juliana gave her a small smile. "I wanted to check in on you to make sure *you* are well."

A smile touched the new dowager's lips as she reached her hand to Juliana's face. Lady Berkshire cupped Juliana's cheek, wiping at a stray tear. Juliana wondered at how she had any left as she sat up straight, wiping at her own face with her palm.

"You have always had a tender heart. Whoever captures it had better keep it safe."

"I am sure I will not have a problem with Peter to help. He shall scare away any tyrant who might come my way." Juliana remembered too late. Peter would not be in London this season. Lady Berkshire's smile broadened.

"I am sure Peter will do a fine job, making sure your beaus are up to snuff. You shall not be afraid to bring him home to meet your father. He will probably be worse than ten blood brothers!"

"You're probably right," Juliana chuckled. "Between him and father, I am doomed to die a spinster."

Lady Berkshire's smile dimmed, and the light faded from her eyes. Juliana cursed inwardly at her poor choice of words. "I am sorry. That was insensitive." Juliana rushed to correct her mistake.

Lady Berkshire leaned over to place a kiss on Juliana's head. "I need your spirit. We will greatly miss you when you leave us behind."

"I shall return home."

"Oh, my dear, I'm afraid you will be snatched up all too quickly. You are so lovely, and we will lose a vital part of our family when you marry."

Juliana pushed back the lump in her throat. This woman was like a mother to her. "I promise to find someone who resides in Newbury so I will be close."

Lady Berkshire smiled. "Be sure to follow your heart, and all will work out for you."

It surprised Juliana at how astute Lady Berkshire was. She'd never dared tell anyone her hopes at finding a love match, not even Peter. Especially not Peter. He would make a joke of it, surely. But the idea had always been there, abstract as it was. She sucked in her breath at the thought.

"I could wait another year. Father would be elated." Her happiness was squashed at the thought of it. She would gladly sacrifice another year. In fact, she wished it now. Anything to lessen Lady Berkshire's grief.

"You most certainly will not." Lady Berkshire came to life. "After all the work, convincing your father to let you go? Death is always with us, Juliana. Life is to be lived. You never know when it will end so grab happiness when you can. I have my memories and Peter. It's time you make some of your own."

Juliana nodded, giving Lady Berkshire a kiss. The door opened and Peter slipped through, smiling at the sight of her kneeling next to his mother. His eyes softened as he moved into the room.

"I loathe to separate my two favorite women but your father is looking for you, Juliana. I fear he is quite worried."

"Thank you, my lady." Juliana stood, then retreated towards the door. She didn't want her father to worry, not at a time like this. Peter caught her hand before she could leave, startled at his quick movement. He brought her hand to his lips, kissing it lightly.

"Thank you again," he whispered.

Her heart caught at the gesture and, throwing convention to the wind, she wrapped her arms around him. He brought her close without hesitation, giving her a squeeze before loosening his grip. He let her go, no longer smiling as she moved from the room. Things were changing, their childhood had slipped away.

He had new responsibilities that she would not be part of and he would now need a wife. An ache settled in her stomach. Even if Peter were to come to London, things would naturally change. They would be forced to change. Though she felt differently.

Peter was *not* her brother.

CHAPTER 4

JULIANA'S AUNT was a practical woman, and Juliana once thought her a bit of a bore. Her aunt would much rather stay at home reading a good book than to socialize. Her uncle was an outgoing, cheerful, sociable soul who often spent his time calling on friends and acquaintances. Despite their differences, they seemed content with each other.

Since her aunt rarely went to social parties, she had designed to take tea with Lady Hawthorn and introduce her to her daughter Patience.

"I think you'll find Miss Hawthorn a delightful girl, not proud like her mother who insists on being addressed as Lady Hawthorn. Though her husband is only a baronet, not even a peer, even so, she will not let you forget that distinction."

Juliana repressed a giggle. She would be glad of any

acquaintance. Since she had arrived, she accompanied her Uncle Henry to events where she was often left to fend for herself while he took to the card rooms or loitered with other elderly gentlemen. Hardly the husband material she wanted to become acquainted with. Rather unconventional, but it was the best she had until now, she hoped.

The carriage pulled to a stop before a line of white row houses. Her aunt rapped on the carriage door with her cane. A footman climbed down from his seat, quickly opened the door and took her card. Stepping to the door of number nineteen, he rapped on the knocker. An elderly butler took the offered card and disappeared inside.

"I hope Lady Hawthorn is in. Such a nuisance roaming the streets, just for a fifteen-minute call."

Juliana peered out the window, and willed the lady to be at home, sending up a silent prayer. She couldn't continue to follow her uncle for surely it would ruin her, a laughingstock to be pitied. Guilt ran through her the moment it entered her head. Hadn't they sacrificed their peace by taking her into their home?

The door opened, and the butler appeared, nodding to the footman.

"There, my dear, you shall have your introduction," her aunt sounded as the footman opened the carriage door.

"Lady Hawthorn is home, ma'am."

They walked up the steps and followed the butler to a small parlor at the front of the house. "Mrs. Gibbon, my lady." He backed out of the room, closing the door behind him.

"My lady, you are so gracious to see us." Her aunt turned into a pillar of etiquette before her eyes as she gave Lady Hawthorn a curtsy fit for a royal.

"May I introduce my niece, Miss Juliana Gibbon. It is her first season, and I thought you should be her first introduction as you are the cream of society."

Lady Hawthorn nodded as if it was her due. "Miss Gibbon, it's nice to meet you. My daughter, Miss Patience Hawthorn."

"Nice to meet you, Miss Hawthorn." Juliana bobbed to the pretty brunette who appeared to be her age, taking a seat beside her.

Her aunt was proficient in keeping Lady Hawthorn's attention while she spoke with the daughter.

"It is your first season?"

"Yes, my father had a difficult time letting me leave him. But my neighbor, Lady Berkshire, convinced him it was time."

"You know Lord Berkshire?" Patience said in awe.

"Yes," Juliana bowed her head, twisting her glove. "The family is in mourning."

"Oh, I am sorry."

"Good day, my lady." Her aunt rose. "Juliana, we must be off."

Fifteen minutes flew by too quickly. Juliana stood, hoping to see Miss Hawthorn again.

"We shall be attending Lady Allen's ball tomorrow night. I hope you will come," Miss Hawthorn smiled.

"Do we have other calls?" Juliana hoped, climbing back into her aunt's carriage.

"Heavens no, one is enough." Her aunt sat back against the seat. "Do not fret my dear, Miss Hawthorn is a virtuous young lady, her mother protects her like a hawk. She will do nicely. How did you find her?"

"Very well on first acquaintance. She will attend the Lady Allen's ball tomorrow."

"Excellent, she will make the introductions for you. I feel you two will be friends."

Juliana tugged on her uncle's sleeve. "Remember Uncle Henry, you must introduce me to our hostess." Juliana insisted as they arrived at the ball. She eyed a group of girls who giggled amongst themselves while their eyes roamed the gentlemen dispersed throughout the room.

"Lady Allen, may I introduce my niece, Miss Juliana Gibbon? This is her first season."

"Then you must introduce Miss Gibbon to the young ladies. If you need an introduction, I will gladly introduce you. My daughter is just over there." Lady

Allen gave Juliana a sympathetic smile that quickly turned down again.

Juliana nodded to the group of ladies across the room. "Over there, Uncle, I believe one of them is Lady Allen's daughter."

He pulled up his quizzing glass to spy on the girls in question. "The one with blonde curls and green dress is the daughter of our hostess. I believe the daughter's name is Rebecca. Same age as you, and the last of her offspring to need a match."

"Let's not waste any time then." She linked arms with her uncle as he led her to the young ladies, eager to make friends. They turned toward Juliana as they approached, and Miss Hawthorn smiled in recognition.

"Good evening, ladies," Uncle Henry said with a bow. "May I have the pleasure of introducing my niece, Juliana Gibbon? This is her first season and she's eager to make friends."

"Good evening." Rebecca's polite demeanor intrigued Juliana, for she felt this girl did not seem to like her. "Do tell us where you hail from?"

Her Uncle Henry, satisfied that he had done his duty, bowed out of the conversation, leaving her with the four young ladies.

"Benham Park, just west of Newbury in Berkshire," Juliana replied. "It borders Alder Court if you've heard of it."

Rebecca's eyes widened. "I have indeed. It's a pity the new Lord Berkshire is not attending the season."

Patience barely concealed her annoyance at Rebecca's change in demeanor. "You are only sorry because he's now a wealthy earl," she said, confirming Juliana's assessment.

Juliana choked back a laugh at the girl's comment. Rebecca spun on her friend, narrowing her eyes. "Patience, one day you'll end up with some penniless fool and wonder why you didn't aim for higher prospects."

Patience raised a brow. "Miss Gibbon, my I introduce Rebecca Allen. Her mother is hosting this ball. Careful, Rebecca, Miss Gibbon will begin to question your character." She gave Juliana a conspiratorial smile. "Tell me, is Lord Berkshire more handsome now that he is an earl?"

Juliana knew she would like Patience as she held back a giggle. "No. In fact, he may become a hunchback from the burden of his newfound responsibility. Would that be worth the fortune?" She turned to the cat-like hostess.

Rebecca looked to the other girls beside her. "I believe I am being goaded. Come, let us take a walk around the room until they can behave as they ought to their host."

The moment Rebecca and her friends were out of

earshot, Juliana and Patience burst into a fit of giggles. "She can be deplorable, but she is entertaining," Patience said, regaining her composure. "Please call me Patience."

"I'm Juliana."

"I know we will be fast friends." Patience giggled.

Juliana's cheeks burned with mirth. "I fear I've made a terrible first impression."

"Just compliment her later, and all will be forgotten. It's her mother you've got to worry about."

"Lady Allen?" Juliana wondered at the hostess as she looked towards the lady. Her back, ramrod straight, looked commanding, as if she knew her worth in society. Juliana wondered if she would ever be able to display such confidence.

Patience nodded as the laughter in her voice disappeared. "Her sole purpose in life is to match her daughter with the most eligible bachelor—and she plays unfair." Patience lowered her voice. "I've heard she once soiled a girl's reputation just so she could marry off her eldest to a duke. Apparently, the other girl was a threat."

Juliana covered her mouth with her fan. "She didn't!"

"Those are the rumors. Rebecca denies it of course, said the poor girl ruined her own reputation. But I wouldn't put it past Lady Allen to have had a secretive hand in it."

"That is deplorable."

"Some matchmaking mamas are absolute monsters," Patience agreed.

Monster or not, Juliana was beginning to feel vile for talking about their host in such a way. "You are not after a title, I presume?"

"Title? What does a title have to do with my happiness?" Patience scoffed, fingering one of her dark curls.

Juliana's interest piqued. "You sound as if you already have a suitor."

"I did once." Patience voice grew soft. "He works as a barrister now. He asked for my hand last year, but my parents refused him because of frivolous things like title, status, and fortune." She shook her head. "I will never love another man as I love Walter Longman."

"What is wrong with a barrister? Working for a living is honorable." Juliana wondered that so small a reason would stop a marriage. "A man of the law can make good connections and a decent wage."

"Decent, exactly," Patience huffed. "But not enough for my parents. I still hate them for refusing Walter. One day perhaps they'll see how unhappy I am without him."

"I'm sorry." Juliana didn't know how to comfort her new friend. She had never been in love before, other than her father and friends, but that wasn't the same as loving a man. Was it? She only had an abstract idea of how wonderful it might be.

Patience shrugged. "Enough about me. Do you have your heart set on anyone?"

Juliana knew Patience was putting on a strong front for her, and she didn't want to intrude on her new friend's confidence. "No. I am hoping to make more acquaintances here in London. I'm afraid I don't know any of the gentlemen in attendance besides my uncle."

"I must introduce you then!" Patience took Juliana's hand as she looked about the room. "Come, you must meet Mr. Westcott. He's adequately charming, and the matchmaking mommas are staying away from him this year because he's the *second* son of Viscount Highfield and there are much bigger fish to catch this season. I feel sorry for his poor brother. He's absolutely *swarmed* by women."

Patience led Juliana toward a handsome, dark-haired gentleman. His brown eyes glittered with mirth as he spoke with another gentleman. His eyes shifted and found Juliana's in an instant.

Patience stopped, his smile moving to her. "I'd like to introduce you to my new friend, Miss Juliana Gibbon. Juliana, this is—"

"James Westcott at your service," he said, bowing lightly, making it feel like a grand gesture.

She followed with a slight curtsy, looking him in the eye. "It's a pleasure to meet you, Mr. Westcott."

"No, Miss Gibbon, the pleasure's all mine." His eyes

sparkled as he looked, appreciatively. Juliana wasn't sure if she should be shy of his assessment.

"Juliana has just arrived in London," Patience said. "From Newbury."

Juliana nodded. "Yes. My arrival was delayed because I stayed behind to attend the funeral of a dear friend."

"The late Lord Berkshire?" Patience inquired.

"Yes, Peter's—I mean Lord Berkshire's father."

Mr. Westcott tilted his head. "You are acquainted with the Seton family?"

"I am. My father's estate borders Alder Court. Lord Berkshire and I grew up together." She knew Peter, his every habit at home at least, but she was beginning to wonder if she knew this new gentleman of society.

"He's all the ladies talk about of late," Mr. Westcott said. "They're waiting an introduction to the new earl. The rumor is he's worth ten thousand a year."

"Perhaps, but Lord Berkshire's fortune isn't his only quality," Juliana admonished. She didn't like the idea that people only liked Peter for his wealth. "He's put up with my silliness and still deems to call me friend. Any young lady would be fortunate to become his countess."

Patience raised her brows. "Including yourself, perhaps?"

Juliana burst into laughter. Several people turned at her outburst, quickly silencing her chortling. "Pet—

Lord Berkshire is like a brother to me. I am not intended for him, nor do I want to be."

Mr. Westcott chuckled. "That boorish, is he?"

"Absolutely not. Have you met him?"

"I'm afraid I have not had the pleasure, but what I hear from the ladies, I may not need to meet him to form an opinion about his character."

"Oh?" Juliana asked, her interest piqued. "What do they say?"

"Some say he is a bit snobbish keeping away from London this year. Others rave about how gallant he is, as if he were a knight-errant."

Juliana eyes crinkled. "His father just passed, and he is mourning. How could they call him a snob for something that is expected? As for gallantry, I suppose he has some of those qualities. But he's no knight-errant, I'm afraid. He doesn't have the daring spirit of a knight."

Patience laughed, and Mr. Westcott nodded thoughtfully. "You've made an intriguing study of this Lord Berkshire. Tell me, what can you glean from me?" He stood straight, placing fingers on his chin, raising his brows comically.

Juliana bit back her laughter. "Having only exchanged a few words with you, I can guess that you have a natural charm around the ladies and gentlemen alike. You find pleasure in unconventional conversation and don't mind gossip—in fact, I'd rather say you crave it."

Mr. Westcott's eyes gleamed. "Impressive. I suppose time will tell if your opinion of me will change."

An older, slightly balding man dressed in the fine clothes, though he looked like a stuffed sausage, sauntered up to Mr. Westcott, bowing to Juliana and Patience. "Mr. Westcott, I find you in the company of two very handsome ladies. Pray, may I beg an introduction?"

"Why, Pincock, I didn't see you arrive. Of course, of course." Mr. Westcott motioned toward them.

Juliana curtsied as Mr. Westcott obliged. "Lord Danbury, may I introduce Miss Patience Hawthorn and Miss Juliana Gibbon. Miss Hawthorn, Miss Gibbon, meet Silas Pincock, the Baron of Danbury."

Juliana studied the man curiously. If these were the prospects this season, she would stay away from catching a title.

"And most unmarried," Lord Danbury added loudly, eyeing both Patience and Juliana. Juliana hid her displeasure. *She* certainly wasn't going to marry this old *Pincock* of a man, even if he was a wealthy peer.

Mr. Westcott laughed awkwardly. "As am I, Lord Danbury."

Lord Danbury clapped Mr. Westcott on the back. "You'll be married soon enough. I am on the prowl for my fourth wife." He turned to Juliana with a bow.

"Would you do me the honor of joining me in the next set?"

Juliana shuddered at forming a connection with the old man, but knew it would be offensive to decline. "I would be honored, Lord Danbury," she grimaced. The man didn't seem to notice as he took her offered hand.

Mr. Westcott turned. "Perhaps you'll save the next for me, Miss Gibbon?"

"I will, thank you." She smiled as Lord Danbury led her onto the dance floor. The scent of rancid candle wax wafted around the man, but she resisted wrinkling her nose as the set began. She should be grateful she had caught the eye of a wealthy man, but she would have preferred her first dance to be with Mr. Westcott.

She craned her neck, searching for Patience as she moved through the steps of the dance. Her gaze fell on Rebecca, who glared as if Juliana had insulted the girl's entire family. Patience and Mr. Westcott danced and conversed not far away. She caught Mr. Westcott's eye and smiled.

"You are lithe on your feet, Miss Gibbon. Do you dance often?" Lord Danbury's comment brought her attention back to him.

"I often attend the parties at the Setons in Newbury. Lady Berkshire is a very social creature."

"I heard about the late Lord Berkshire. How is Lady Berkshire faring?"

"Decidedly less social, as you can imagine. She is mourning and will be for quite some time."

Lord Danbury nearly shouted every phrase he uttered in a booming voice as they made small talk. She wondered if he might be slightly hard of hearing, sighing with relief when the set ended, bringing her back to her friends.

Patience giggled as Lord Danbury retreated. "Has he made an offer of marriage yet? Or promised to make you wealthy?" Patience teased.

Juliana cast her eyes to the ceiling before it was too late. "Hardly. I should be pleased never to dance with the gentleman again."

Mr. Westcott's brows shot up. "That enjoyable, was it?"

"It was *that* enjoyable," Juliana teased.

"Shall we?" Mr. Westcott laughed, offering his arm as the next set started.

He swept her away, easily maneuvering her into place. "Lord Danbury complimented me on my lightness of foot," Juliana teased.

"I daresay he's right. You're a better dancer than my younger sister. She has two left feet."

"You have a sister?"

"Yes, and an elder brother." His affable grin disguised a slight note of annoyance.

"I envy you."

"Why so?" Mr. Westcott's smile widened. "Do you have any siblings?"

"I am afraid not. My mother has been dead these past twelve years, so my father likes to keep me close, which is why I am just now coming to London."

"I am sorry for that. I should have liked to meet you sooner."

"It's not as bad as it seems. Lady Berkshire has been like a second mother."

Something changed in Mr. Westcott's eyes. Was it envy?

"I shall enjoy another dance with you very much." Mr. Westcott moved away into the next step. Juliana found she liked Mr. Westcott.

CHAPTER 5

JULIANA DIPPED her pen in the ink well and scratched out the formal heading. It had been almost six months since Peter's father died, and she still wasn't used to Peter's title. Would she ever fit in completely with this crazy society where titles mattered?

She hadn't been schooled from Debrett's Peerage of England because her father wasn't concerned with her marriage. Had her mother lived, she was sure she would have received a more appropriate education to enter society.

My Dearest Lord, No, that wouldn't do. She started again.

Staring at the blank page. *The Right Honourable Earl of Berkshire*. She giggled at the formal address.

What would Peter think of all the talk about him? Although she missed him, luck had brought her a kindred spirit in Patience. She didn't know what she would have done had she not met her. The gentlemen of the ton weren't what she had expected or hoped. Mr. Westcott seemed to like her, but she wasn't sure. She hadn't formed a firm opinion of him yet. Juliana put pen to parchment again.

As much as it pains me to say this, I despise London. It is crowded and dirty. Most of the girls my age whom I imagined might become new friends, smile and simper with their mouths but their eyes shoot daggers.

I can imagine I might have enjoyed my come out more if you had been here. Now wipe that smile off your face. Don't suppose I want you. I just wonder if the transition would be easier if I could boast an acquaintance with "The most eligible bachelor of the season, The Earl of Berkshire."

Oh, Peter, do you know how often you are talked about? Everyone is speculating as to if you will come this season. It is almost scandalous. Half the time I must force myself not to show my annoyance. As if your title has changed you. You are not your title. You are just Peter, my friend. I cannot understand the aristocracy. It is as if everyone is in a race to secure a title or wealth or both with no regard to compatibility or love.

I do not know what I imagined it would be like, but not this. How can I tell if I am being courted for me, rather than my dowry?

Father has not stamped out my habit of showing my

emotions even if he supposed he had, for I find myself annoyed most often, but Miss Stringham's training is most helpful in public. You will be proud of me.

Why must I be forced to marry? No, that is not right. I do want to marry. It's just that I want to—. Never mind. I am being silly. I shall try harder to find enjoyment in the process, but it is not what I expected.

I do enjoy dancing, and there is one potential interest. His name is Mr. James Westcott. He is the second son of the Viscount of Highfield, which of course makes him slightly unworthy of the more ambitious mommas this season. I wonder if the only reason I like him is because all the mothers are vying for Mr. Pincock, the Baron of Danbury. Oh, Peter, he is so old! And he smells of rancid candle wax. I am not lying. He does, and I am wracking my brain as to why.

I am being silly again. I suppose that means I should let you go. Do not worry about me. I will only accept someone I am fond of and who makes me laugh.

Yours, Juliana

Peter smiled as he read Juliana's letter. Checked himself and read it again. It was a ray of sunshine in the gloom of Alder Court. His mother grieved heavily while he had taken up his father's affairs. He still missed him with each passing day. He felt useless as of late. His mother needed more time to heal, and he found himself lonely after six months. The only people to visit were elderly gentlemen and their wives, offering their condolences and remarking on the fine weather they'd been having lately. It was hardly stimulating conversation, and most of his friends were in London.

He leaned on his chin, scanning Juliana's letter again. He should have guessed Juliana would hate London — she preferred running through the wild of their properties. Riding, practicing archery, or sitting by his lake feeding the ducks. He smiled, thinking back to her insistence the lake belonged to her. He knew now, after going through the books, that the lake belonged to his family.

London was crowded, noisy and had many formal conventions. No, Juliana wouldn't fit in with the ton.

Peter folded the letter and tucked it away in his desk. He made his way to his mother's sitting room where he knew she would be reading, painting, or more often crying. Today she seemed brighter. He approached from behind while she dabbed paint onto her canvas, working on a sprawling landscape. Her eyes darted to him before she refocused on her work.

"Hello Peter." Her voice sounded tired.

"How are you today?" He sat watching the paint hit the canvas.

"Better. I doubt the pain will ever go away, but painting soothes me. Keeps my mind off things." She squinted at a tree to which she had just added leaves. She set down her brush, turning to face him. "How are you feeling?"

"I miss him." Peter's somber tone set the mood.

She nodded, and they lapsed into silence.

Peter cleared his throat. "I've been thinking of going to London for the rest of the season."

"Oh?" His mother picked up her brush, mixing yellow pigment with green.

"Everything is settled here and father's steward has everything in hand." He shifted restlessly. "I think I need a change of scenery."

"I agree." His mother pressed her lips together. The brush in her hand formed a tree as the branches took shape.

"You do?"

"I'm sorry I haven't been enjoyable company lately. You should go to London—find a pretty girl to turn your head. It's time you find a wife. A marriage might distract us both."

Peter grimaced. "I'm not sure I'm ready for marriage." He hesitated, looking into his mother's eyes. "Come to London with me. It will distract your mind from father. It's been six months and your friends will welcome you."

Lady Berkshire sighed. "I am not ready." The corners of her mouth tilted upward. "But you—must go.

I'll be fine here. You know I have support enough for five grieving wives."

Peter lifted the brush from her grasp, setting it aside. He held her hand. "Are you sure?"

"Positive. When can you be ready to leave?"

Peter smiled, giving in to his mother's request. It was clear from Juliana's letters that she needed him and his mother needed more time.

"Tomorrow, I think."

Rebecca snagged Juliana away while Patience chatted with a middle-aged gentleman about exotic fruits. She tucked Juliana's arm against her own and wandered around the crowded ballroom, a sly smile lighting her features.

"I think we started off on the wrong foot, Juliana. I would like to introduce you to my mother. She is so eager to meet you."

Juliana hid her surprise. "That sounds nice," she lied. "How is Lord Danbury? I've seen you two engaged in intimate conversation as of late."

Rebecca smiled, but her eyes hardened. "He is a very clever gentleman, and very rich."

And smells rancid, Juliana thought, repressing a smile. "Yes, it seems he's grown his fortune with each new wife he collects."

Rebecca narrowed her eyes.

"Is your mother keen on marrying you off to him?" Juliana said, instantly cursing herself for being so insensitive.

But Rebecca just laughed. "Yes, but we'll see if we're a match soon enough. Here she is." She held her hand out, gesturing to her mother.

Juliana had studied Lady Allen at London's social events but had never spoken to her other than when they were introduced. She might have been a beautiful woman were it not for her nose that was a little too pointed. Still, her blonde hair was piled up in a fashionable style. Her smirk just like her daughter's, a typical society matron.

"Mother, I'd like to introduce you to a good friend of mine, Juliana Gibbon."

Lady Allen's mirthful eyes turned to Juliana and instantly flitted up and down, taking in her dress, hair, face, bust, and sizing her up as competition, she guessed.

Juliana felt exposed.

"Yes, I remember Miss Gibbon." Lady Allen nodded.

Juliana sunk into a curtsy. "Lady Allen."

Lady Allen sniffed. "From where do you hail Miss Gibbon?"

"Newbury," Juliana straightened. "My father's estate is near Alder Court."

Lady Allen's brows rose. "Oh? You are acquainted with Lord Berkshire, I imagine?"

"Yes, very." Juliana was held in higher esteem just for knowing her dear friend, but she doubted this woman would give her such credit. Something flickered across Lady Allen's face—whether it was jealousy or a brief annoyance, Juliana could not tell.

"It is a shame he is not with us this season," Lady Allen quipped. "I believe he and Rebecca became the best of friends last year—isn't that right, Rebecca?" Lady Allen turned to her daughter, giving her a telling look.

Rebecca laughed. "Mother, I believe you're confusing Lord Berkshire with—" Lady Allen gave her a harsh stare. Rebecca paused. "Yes, Lord Berkshire and I are well acquainted."

"Indeed?" Juliana easily saw through the lie. "I don't believe Lord Berkshire's ever mentioned the fact."

"Lord Berkshire is a private person," Rebecca said, a fake smile playing about her lips. "I don't believe he's mentioned you to me either, Miss Gibbon. Two different worlds, Newbury and London—don't you think, Mother?"

Lady Allen nodded, a pleased look on her face.

Juliana had enough of these games. They were just toying with her to extract information. "I will be sure to give him your regards when I return home." She curtsied. "Excuse me." She walked away, fury burning within her. *Deplorable*. How could Rebecca call her a friend one moment, then treat her as competition the next? She didn't understand this society.

She scanned the room, looking for Patience among the crowd. Her eyes wandered toward the doorway. Her heart fluttered, and her stomach lurched. Peter stood just inside. Honey curls swept away from his forehead. Her heart raced. My, he was handsome. His blue coat trimmed with a black velvet collar fit to perfection. His eyes wandered the room before landing on her. A smile transformed his features. She took a step toward him when Patience appeared before her with arched brows.

"What did Rebecca want?" she asked, her voice eager.

"She introduced me to her mother. You're right—the two were scheming against me because I know the gentleman with a shiny new title. Speaking of which—"

"I can't stand the Allens," Patience groaned. "They're a bad influence on my mother. She's been pushing me toward gentlemen whom I have no interest in. I've just escaped her."

The orchestra finished their number, paused, and started up another, this one slower. Couples retreated and others stepped onto the dance floor, ready to start the next set. Juliana glanced toward the door. Disappointed Peter was no longer there.

"Who are you looking for? Has Mr. Westcott arrived?" Patience followed her eyes around the room.

"Miss Gibbon." Juliana and Patience startled as Peter stood before them, a pleasant smile on his face. "Would you care to dance?" He bowed before her.

Juliana's heart skipped. "Peter you're here… in London." She reached for his offered arm.

"I couldn't miss my favorite lady's first season," he teased.

She giggled, glad to see him. He escorted her to the dance floor, Patience gaping after them.

"I don't understand, I thought you weren't coming to London."

"I wasn't. But the house was so gloomy. I thought the change might brighten my spirits."

"I hope you're prepared to be the center of attention," Juliana teased. "The new Lord Berkshire is all the mommas are talking about."

Peter laughed, stepping around her until they stood face to face. "How are you faring?" Concern flashed across his face.

"Tolerable, if I ignore people studying me." Juliana glanced around the room. Female eyes watched, gauging how much of a threat she was to their chances to grasp the new Lord Berkshire. It was laughable, really, because she posed as much threat as a protective sister.

"How is your mother?" She turned to Peter, ignoring the attention he drew.

"Still in mourning, I'm afraid." Peter took her hand

in his to guide her down the line of dancers. "But I left with her blessing."

"When did you arrive in London?"

"Just today—I received your letter."

"Oh?" Juliana smiled brightly.

"Yes. I must meet this baron you spoke of. Danbury, was it? Perhaps I can help solve this candle wax mystery."

Juliana laughed. How she missed their conversations. She noticed Rebecca and Lady Allen out of the corner of her eye as they swirled across the floor. Lady Allen's eyes were sharp while Rebecca's bottom lip protruded in a pout. The dance ended and Juliana curtsied while Peter bowed, before taking her arm.

"You must introduce me to your new friends."

"Oh, I must introduce you to Patience. She has been the single joy I've found while here in London."

They found Patience standing next to her mother, who patted her elbow and nodded toward them as she whispered in her ear. Patience's lips pressed tightly together.

"Patience," Juliana called as they reached her, "this is—"

"Lord Berkshire, I'm pleased to make your acquaintance," Patience curtsied. "You are not at all the hunchback Juliana made you out to be."

Peter threw a look at Juliana, his brow cocked.

Juliana grinned. "I only meant it metaphorically.

Someone had to bring these ladies to their senses. They talked of you as if you were an angel sent from heaven to rescue them from misfortune," she giggled.

"Lord Berkshire, may I introduce Lady Hawthorn? Lady Hawthorn, Peter Seton, the Earl of Berkshire."

"I am honored, my lord." Lady Hawthorn gave Peter a deep curtsy as if he were the king.

"Sounds like you've been up to no good in my absence," Peter whispered. But the light chastisement fell on deaf ears.

Juliana caught site of Rebecca making her way toward them.

"Oh no, here comes your greatest admirer. Quick, Peter, dance with Patience."

Peter glanced back, but Juliana grasped his hand and placed it in Patience's.

Peter frowned. "You're being childish," he quipped, dropping Patience hand.

"Would you do me the honor, Miss Patience?"

"The honor's all mine." Patience giggled.

"Go, go." Juliana shooed them away.

Patience's mother cast her an approving smile, but Juliana watched the couple as Peter led Patience further onto the dance floor, unaware of brushing past Rebecca. He hadn't caught sight of her or didn't know who she was.

Rebecca wandered over and her attention turned to Juliana. "It seems Lord Berkshire has granted us a surprise visit." Rebecca's artificial smile irritated Juliana.

"It seems he has," Juliana focused her attention on her friends.

"He must have heard us talking about him," Rebecca said.

Juliana was in no mood to be friendly with Rebecca. She spotted Mr. Westcott entering the ballroom. "Excuse me," she muttered and walked toward the gentleman.

"Mr. Westcott," she curtsied. "It's good to see you here."

"I hope I am not too late." He gave her a slight bow.

"Not at all. Just in time in fact. My friend Lord Berkshire has just arrived."

"Has he?" Mr. Westcott's brow rose.

"Indeed. You see, he is dancing with Patience. It appears Miss Allen is eager to dance with him as well." Rebecca stood, biting her lip as she watched the dancers.

Mr. Westcott laughed. "Lord Berkshire will not be able to escape the attention of every young lady or their mothers here tonight." He offered an arm to Juliana. "Would you dance with me, Miss Gibbon?"

Juliana grinned, placing her hand in the crook of Mr. Westcott's arm. "Absolutely." Her smile was genuine.

Juliana did not speak with Peter the rest of the evening, as Mr. Westcott's predictions had been true.

Rebecca did eventually dance with Peter, along with many other eager ladies who were introduced by their mommas.

Peter's eyes often found hers throughout the evening. He looked weary from all the conversation and dancing. She smiled back and enjoyed the company of her friends. A twisted part of her delighted in his social torment. It was payback for the years of teasing. But she was immensely grateful for his appearance in London.

CHAPTER 6

JULIANA ARRIVED at Patience's London townhome, only a short walk from where she was staying with her aunt and uncle, while her maid walked a small distance behind. Patience's family was very well off, taking the best house in Grosvenor Square. With so much wealth, why not let Patience marry for love?

Her friend was already at the door, donning her gloves and checking her bonnet.

"Patience, you are ready for our walk!"

"I could not wait to hear the gossip about your Lord Berkshire. We had a pleasant conversation. He talked of you often."

Juliana did not miss the cunning glint in Patience's eye as they set out toward Hyde Park. Patience's maid stepped next to Juliana's as they followed behind.

"I think I counted at least five gentlemen eager to

make your acquaintance the other night." Patience chuckled. "You'll find yourself with a rich husband before the season ends!"

"Pray, faith!" Juliana took her eyes heavenward. "I would not dream of courting the half of them."

Patience brow raised. "And what of Mr. Westcott? You two click like you've known each other for years."

It was true that Juliana had grown fond of Mr. Westcott, even if it seemed he tried a little too hard to match her wit. He was a kind gentleman and didn't mind if she toed conventional lines at times. In fact, he seemed to enjoy her frank humor and freely given mirth.

"Mr. Westcott is a sweet soul. But I have not formed any opinions as far as courtship is concerned." She took Patience's arm in hers. "What about you? Peter seems to enjoy your company as much as I do."

"Yes," Patience said slowly, "Although—I still think of Walter. I cannot imagine being with another man. I'd rather die an old maid."

"Come now. There is more than one amiable man in the country."

Patience chewed at her bottom lip. "My mother wants me to pursue Lord Berkshire."

Juliana's chest constricted at the thought. "And will you?"

Patience laughed, lightening the mood. "Of course not. But she won't stop pestering me until I show some interest."

"And Peter won't stop being chased by other women," Juliana whispered thoughtfully. A smile cracked her face as an idea came to her.

"What is it? What's on that devious mind of yours?"

Juliana nearly skipped with scheming excitement. "You should let Peter court you."

Patience shifted uncomfortably. "But I've already said I don't want to."

"No—you and Peter should *pretend* to court," Juliana revised in a whisper. "That way, your mother will relax, and Peter will be able to enjoy the rest of the season in peace." She looked back to her maid to see if they had been overheard. They were safe as the maids were out of earshot.

Patience gave Juliana a sidelong glance. "That's ridiculous. My mother would expect a marriage proposal."

"Which Peter will give," Juliana said as giddy excitement bubbled up, replacing her earlier jealousy. "Of which you will refuse."

Patience groaned. "My parents would kill me. No my mother would and I'd become a social outcast."

"Just tell them you tried to love another man but couldn't forget your dear Mr. Longman. If they have any heart, they might accept that."

The girls circled a stark, old trunk of a tree which Juliana supposed was an elm.

"I don't think this will work and I am sure Lord Berkshire would never agree."

"Come now, it will be great fun. It might take your mind off your barrister, even if for just a little while," Juliana urged. "Let me take care of Peter, you two converse so well. It won't take much convincing to spread some rumors that Peter is courting you."

"I suppose it would keep my mother from badgering me about finding a suitor for a few weeks." Patience nibbled her lip.

"Any woman with sense would back off Peter when they learn he is courting." Juliana didn't know why that thought gave her such comfort. "Although, I have to admit it has been great fun watching his discomfort."

"Why don't *you* court him then?" Patience eyebrows lifted.

"Because." Juliana searched her mind for a valid reason. "Because the ruse would not benefit me as it would you."

"All right, if Peter agrees to it, I will too." They turned to exit the park.

Juliana's smile stretched, excitement pushing out any rational thought warning her this was a bad idea, and headed for Patience's home, impatient to start their ruse.

"You want me to do what?" Peter asked, sure he had misunderstood.

Juliana sat in front of him in her uncle's parlor, Patience blushing beside her.

Juliana's smile grew wider. "Poor Patience needs a respite from her controlling mother. If you pretended to court her—"

Peter huffed out a laugh of disbelief. "This is a bad idea, Juliana." He looked to Patience. "I'm sorry to disappoint you, Miss Patience."

She smiled, not looking disappointed at all. "I am not, it was a wild idea." She gave Juliana a shrug.

"It's not wild! Peter, you're being pestered by ladies in your time of grief. This could give you the distance you need. Plus, I can't wait to see Rebecca's face when she learns you're courting Patience." Juliana clapped her hands.

Peter leaned forward, locking eyes with her. "I do not make a habit of pretending around my friends." He glared sternly at her, sure now that she had gone mad.

Juliana clenched her jaw. "It would just be for a few weeks till the end of the season."

Peter sighed and looked to Patience. "And what will happen when I am expected to make an offer? What then?"

"I would refuse it," Patience blurted. She glanced at Juliana. "There's a hope that my refusal to you and my commitment to Mr. Longman will secure my parents' blessing—this time." The pain in Patience's eyes caused Peter to soften.

This fit Juliana's personality. She was loyal to a fault, and now she seemed to have taken on Miss Hawthorn's plight.

Peter lowered his eyes to his hands. If this was simply a scheme to convince Patience's parents to let her marry the man she loved—he shook his head. No matter the wrapping, it still sounded like a foolhardy business.

"I'm not going along with this Juliana," he stated firmly.

She frowned. "You, Lord Berkshire, are no fun."

"And you have too much of it," Peter countered. "At other people's expense, I might add."

"The only expense would be your own, Lord Berkshire, with all due respect," Patience broke in, loyalty to her friend pushing past her earlier discomfort. "Juliana is only trying to help the both of us have a more enjoyable season."

Peter pressed his lips together, trying to calm his unease. "And if I decide I'd like to court another young lady?"

Juliana shrugged. "Then we'll end the scheme. Patience will renounce your intentions." Her friend nodded beside her.

He still didn't like it, but he also didn't like the way Juliana looked at him, expectant. If he said no, he would ruin her high spirits. Besides, he didn't have plans to court anyone... this year… yet.

"All right," Peter sighed. Against his better judgment. He locked eyes with Patience and stood, bowing low and taking her soft hand in his. "Miss Patience, I would like to court you under the guise of protecting both you and me from unwanted romantic interests. As soon as I make an offer, you are to refuse. I reserve the right to end this fake courtship any time I choose. Are we in agreement?"

Patience smiled, her cheeks growing slightly pink again. "We are," she brightened.

Peter squeezed her hand lightly before straightening and turning to Juliana. Her eyes were bright with merriment.

"Someday, some poor gentleman will have to deal with your demands for the rest of his life," he said wryly.

"For the time being, that unfortunate gentleman will have to be you," she returned with a giggle.

He suddenly had the urge to repent of this scheme and wash his hands of the whole business. But Juliana's shining eyes gave him pleasure he was not expecting. Despite his earlier teasing, the man who caught her affections would be a very happy man indeed.

"Come now, you must take us to Gunter's for some of their famous ice. I have not yet been but have heard the most delicious things about it," Juliana persuaded.

"Because I do not have a stack of things to do already," Peter said dryly.

"Come, you came to London to enjoy its pleasures and forget about your new responsibilities. This will be the perfect start to your courtship."

Peter held his arm for Patience, a smile forming as he did so. "Miss Patience, I would be honored if you would accompany me to Gunter's. You may invite your friend along if you desire." His smile was barely concealed, and he could see Juliana beaming from the corner of his eye.

Patience gave him a grin before taking his offered hand, letting him help her from the settee she shared with Juliana.

The ladies made ready, and he stepped onto the street, a lady on each arm. The walk was just a seven-minute stroll, but they caught the eyes of many as they paraded down the crowded streets of his summer residence.

This woman would be the death of him. He gazed at Juliana, her blonde curls poking from under her pretty new bonnet. How was it that she could so easily persuade him? He'd never had this problem before. *You've never seen her as a woman before*, a voice inside chided.

He turned his attention to Patience as they neared Gunter's Tea shop, resolved to pay as much attention to

Juliana's friend as possible. No one would ever accuse him of shirking his duties.

Waiters started across the street to open carriages where people were dressed to show off their gowns, bringing them their ice and other treats. The patrons rested under the shade of trees, wanting to be seen instead of going inside to mingle. There were many people Peter knew already outside. It seemed Gunter's was a popular spot for the beau monde. He stepped into the tea shop, scanning the room for people he might know when a waiter ran to them, guiding them to a small table. The crowded shop smelled of confections.

Juliana took a seat next to Patience. He slipped in next to her as she watched the waiters bring molded ice, shaped as various fruits, to other guests. The outside of the glass was lightly frosted, causing it to look refreshing.

"This place is packed with the cream of society." Juliana brought her focus to Peter in wide-eyed excitement.

"It is one of the few acceptable places to sit with a gentleman and dine in public. And the food is exceptional," Peter offered.

"You sound as if you've already enjoyed the delicacy." Juliana studied him, a new look of interest forming in her curious eyes.

"I brought my mother," he said quickly, avoiding the subject of his previous season's admirers. He had no idea why the thought of her knowing his former attempts at lovemaking rattled him.

"I've had them too." Patience joined the conversation. "The pineapple ice is the best, but they don't always have it available."

Juliana turned to her friend. "I would love to try the pineapple. I have never tasted its flavor."

"Oh, you will love it. The cream in the ice makes it smooth on the palate," Patience smiled broadly.

A waiter stopped at their table. "Are you ready to order, my lord?" There was no trace of a guttural accent as he spoke.

Peter turned to Juliana. "Would you like to try the pineapple?"

"If they have it." She smiled.

He nodded before turning his attention to Patience. "Do you know what you would like?" he asked with an adoring smile.

A slight blush colored Patience's cheek. "I'll have the raspberry," she said quickly, turning her attention to Juliana.

He turned back to the waiter. "Two pineapple ice and one raspberry. I would also like a plate of Shrewsbury cakes."

Juliana scolded, "You still have a penchant for Shrewsbury cakes?"

"Indeed. They are better than the biscuits."

Patience broke in, defending Peter. "The Shrewsbury cake goes very well with the ice."

"I will have to take your word as I have never had them," Juliana smiled at her friend.

Peter instantly knew she was just trying to tease him. How the tables had turned.

The waiter departed, and Juliana cried in delight as Mr. Westcott moved his way to their table.

"I find myself astonished to spy you in here as I walked past. I just had to come inside to see how you are enjoying London."

"Do sit and join us, Mr. Westcott." Juliana smiled and pointed to a seat next to Peter.

"I don't wish to intrude."

"Nonsense. We would love to have your company. Isn't that right, Lord Berkshire?" She turned her expectant eyes to Peter.

He nodded in agreement. "Of course, relax with us. It is Juliana's first time visiting Gunter's." Peter felt annoyance at being joined by Mr. Westcott. With Peter supposedly courting Patience, it would mean Mr. Westcott could give his attention to Juliana. The thought did not sit well with him.

Mr. Westcott pulled out the last remaining seat, sitting next to Peter *and* Juliana. Mr. Westcott turned his chair toward Juliana. "How do you enjoy London?"

"It wasn't what I expected. Saving your good

company, and of course Patience, I'm not sure I would have survived."

Peter looked affronted. "What am I, chopped liver? I rushed to London to save you from the bane of society, and this is the thanks I get!" He was only half jesting.

"I meant before you came to London." Her laughing eyes returned to Mr. Westcott.

He returned her smile with an affectionate grin. "You are old news, I dare say, at least where Miss Gibbon is concerned. With the new title, I'm sure you'll find more suitable admirers. Can't have them all, good man," he joked to Peter.

Juliana turned excitedly to Mr. Westcott, bringing him in on their secret. "Lord Berkshire has his eyes on Miss Patience."

Patience's eyes widened. Peter placed his hand over Patience to comfort her at the announcement. She was probably not prepared for the sudden reveal of the game.

"Really? Quite extraordinary." Mr. Westcott seemed truly surprised.

"Yes, well, it was my mother's idea. She's got it in her mind that a wife would bring some much-needed sunshine to Alder Court. Can't argue with a grieving widow." Peter did not like having his actions open to scrutiny, especially by this man who so clearly had an interest in Juliana.

"You mustn't blame poor Lord Berkshire. Patience

really is extraordinary and very charming," Juliana defended him.

Mr. Westcott nodded at Juliana's explanation. Compared to Juliana, Patience paled, though she was beautiful in her own right.

"I find Miss Hawthorn's charms to be enchanting." Peter smiled at Patience.

Patience seemed to lighten, giving him a small smile as the refreshments were placed before them.

"You must order some ice for yourself," Juliana turned to Mr. Westcott.

"No, I was on my way to my club when I spied you through the window."

Juliana turned to the waiter. "Will you please bring an extra spoon?"

"Sharing your dessert isn't the thing," Peter scolded.

The waiter promptly returned, placing the extra spoon in front of Mr. Westcott. "I know we are not in the country, but do you not think it bad manners to eat in front of friends?" Juliana scooted her ice, so it lay in between her and Mr. Westcott.

Mr. Westcott chuckled slightly. "Far be it from me to deny our Miss Gibbon. Perhaps I will just take a taste." He took a small wedge from her ice before tasting the sweet concoction and placing the spoon in front of him.

"Now Miss Gibbon, do not let me interfere with the pleasure of your ice. Go ahead and enjoy the rest." He slid the ice back to Juliana with a pleased smile on his lips.

Did Juliana realize the tone she was sending Mr. Westcott? It was tantamount to a pursuit, and the gentleman didn't seem to mind.

He focused his attention on Patience as he took a bite of his ice. But Juliana's happy enthusiasm toward her ice made it hard for him to concentrate on his *intended* for long.

When the treats were eaten, and the conversation waned, Peter helped Patience from the table. Taking her arm, they took the lead. Peter forced his thoughts to menial matters as Julianna tittered behind, hanging on Westcott's every word. He pushed away the discomfort it brought and refocused his efforts on playing his part.

CHAPTER 7

PETER WALKED into the brightly lit assembly. The noise of laughter and chatter buzzing in his ears. The parties hadn't slowed as the season neared its end. This event was as crowded as ever. He squeezed his way through, scanning the room, looking for Juliana, his anchor, a ray of sunshine he could always look forward to.

Peter noticed Juliana through the crowd wearing a pale blue gown, her light hair pinned up in a becoming style on top of her head. Her eyes met his, and a smile brightened her already pretty face.

A woman stepped into his line of vision blocking his view. He blinked; glancing down, he was met with long feathers extending from neatly coiffured hair. The familiar lady looked to be about twenty years his senior. He couldn't quite place where they'd met, so he politely waited for her to speak.

"Good evening Lord Berkshire." The woman dipped in a small curtsy, giving him a feigned look of sorrow. "May I offer you my deepest condolences?"

"Thank you." He gave a slight bow, annoyed at being distracted from Juliana.

She straightened, scanning his face. "You do not remember me?" she asked with a laugh, her features instantly changing. "Lady Allen."

Ahh, Miss Allen's mother. The two women shared the same eyes. "Oh yes. Forgive me." He had become acquainted with Miss Allen only briefly last season. The daughter had been pursuing a now-married earl to allow him much attention.

Lady Allen smiled the way a fox would before attacking a coop of hens.

"I wanted to ask a special favor of you tonight." She placed a gloved hand on the arm of his evening coat. "My daughter, Miss Allen, would be delighted if you would reserve a couple dances for her this evening. The poor girl has so many suitors, I believe you would be a breath of fresh air."

Peter knew the trap she was laying. He cleared his throat. "I thank you, Lady Allen, for the kind compliments. But as I hope to spend my time escorting Miss Hawthorn…"

Lady Allen's eyes widened. "How fortunate for Miss Hawthorn." She removed her hand from his arm, placing it to her breast. "But sad for the other young ladies who may not get the chance to dance. Surely you should think of them?"

"I see your point," Peter said carefully. "But clearly your daughter needn't any more attention with so many *suitors* of her own."

Lady Allen's mouth dropped open at Peter's rebuff and he silently cursed himself for being so callous. Juliana's directness must be rubbing off on him. He cleared his throat. "But I understand the social pressures your daughter must be going through. I'll reserve one dance for her," he amended.

Lady Allen's jaw locked. "That is very kind of you, my lord. She will be most grateful."

Peter bowed. "Good evening, Lady Allen."

"Of course, my lord." She retreated, her feathered head held high. He couldn't help thinking she would fit in nicely with the likes of Lord Danbury.

He looked where Juliana had been standing. He had promised to speak with Miss Hawthorn's parents but the thought wasn't as palatable as it had been yesterday. He could see Juliana and Patience laughing with a group of young gentlemen. At least three encircled Juliana and appeared to be enraptured by whatever she was saying. He hadn't realized she'd become so popular. The thought sat heavy in his chest, though he pushed it aside.

Patience was the first to see him. Her smile broadened as he walked their way. She cocked her head.

"Ready to meet my parents?" she whispered, batting her eyelashes dramatically.

"Yes, if we are to continue with this plan of Juliana's," he whispered back.

Juliana moved to Peter and lowered her voice. "Of course we are still going through with it. Otherwise, you'll have more than one Lady Allen on your heels, and Patience may never be able to wed the man she loves."

Peter's brows lifted. "It's all highly irregular," he squirmed, offering Patience his arm...

"Don't you worry, it will only be for a few weeks." Patience placed her hand in the crook of his arm.

"What am I getting myself into?" It was Peter's turn to take his eyes to the ceiling.

Juliana giggled as Patience led him to her parents, who were lounging on chairs in an alcove, chatting with their friends. Patience moved beside her father.

"Father, Lord Berkshire would like to speak with you."

"Heavens above!" Patience's mother stood, stepping to Peter. "Lord Berkshire, it is an honor to see you."

"The honor's all mine." Peter bowed, feeling like a fool in front of this woman who was clearly gushing over his title.

"Lord Berkshire, this is my mother, Lady Hawthorn, and my father, Sir Nicolas." Her father stood.

"'Tis a pleasure to finally meet you," Peter said, taking a slight bow.

"And I you," Mr. Hawthorn said gruffly, darting his eyes to his daughter then back to him. Peter felt he was about to be caught out as a fraud.

An awkward silence ensued in which Patience looked to Peter expectantly. "Lord Berkshire?" she asked. "Is there something you'd like to ask my father?"

Peter cleared his throat. "Yes. Mr. Hawthorn, I have become quite enthralled with your daughter and would like your permission to see more of her, your daughter that is."

Mrs. Hawthorn squealed with excitement. "Yes, yes, you may!" she cried before her husband could speak.

Peter smiled, resisting the urge to loosen his cravat as the room suddenly grew warmer.

Mr. Hawthorn grunted. "Permission to see her? With the intention for what exactly?"

He didn't look pleased. "To see if we get on, sir." Peter felt his tongue go dry, why couldn't he just say it, *to court your daughter*. It seemed so final.

Mrs. Hawthorn giggled, clutching Patience's hands. Patience grinned with her mother, but the light didn't touch her eyes. She was bothered by something. Her mischievous excitement had dimmed.

"Nicolas, can't you see? Lord Berkshire wants to court Patience."

"Is that your intention, Lord Berkshire?" Sir

Hawthorn huffed.

"Yes, sir." Peter slowly nodded. This wasn't going to end well. Patience's reputation would be ruined.

"Well then, you have my permission," Sir Hawthorn relented.

They walked away, Patience's arm limply lying in the crook of his as he led her onto the dance floor.

"Is anything the matter?" Her changed mood heightened his concern. Was she regretting this farce? He certainly was. He felt as if a noose was about his neck and when the truth was found out, he would be hanged. *Here hangs Lord Berkshire, the deceiver of ladies, beware.*

Patience met his eyes, and he saw a slight glimmer. "I just wish they'd shown that level of excitement when Walter asked for my hand in marriage. Or any excitement at all." Her brow knit together.

"I'm sorry."

She pinned on a smile that didn't meet her eyes. "It is not your fault, my lord." She blinked her eyes. "It is behind us now. Shall we enjoy the ball?"

They joined the dancers for the next few sets. Peter noticed Rebecca was always in sight, watching with her big green eyes, reminding him of his promise to her mother.

He thought of his own mother, alone at Alder Court and grieving over her lost husband. His heart twisted, so when the second dance ended, he searched the room for

Juliana. If she hadn't been there, he might have left the ball altogether.

She was using her charming smile on some poor fool. He wondered if she was doing it on purpose. The thought irritated him, and he found himself wondering why. Why should he care that she was enjoying the company of other gentlemen? After all she was here to find her spouse.

"Is something on your mind?" Patience asked.

He gestured toward Juliana. "She has so many admirers."

Patience chuckled. "Yes, Juliana is beautiful and amusing, a lethal combination."

"Does she have an interest in any of them?" Peter asked before he could stop himself.

"Not that I know. She does enjoy Mr. Westcott's company."

Peter escorted Patience off the dance floor groaning inwardly as Rebecca came into view.

"Lord Berkshire?" Patience turned to the voice. Rebecca smiled shyly. "I wasn't sure if you remembered me from last season."

"Yes," he said quickly. "I remember being introduced. I just was speaking with Lady Allen earlier this evening."

Rebecca's eyes trained on him, refusing to let him go. "I offer my sincerest condolences for the passing of your father. Is your mother well?"

"Grieving still, but she has good friends who are seeing to her comfort." Peter didn't wish to discuss the subject, lastly with Rebecca.

"Poor thing." Her voice dripped with fake sympathy. "I hear she is a very social creature. She must be crushed."

Peter's jaw clenched. "Yes, she loved my father very much." It was the same words he'd used over and over for the past months.

"What inspired you to return to London?" Rebecca asked, unaware he wanted to talk of something else. Any other subject. This small talk was so useless. He knew what she was digging for.

Patience dropped Peter's arm and stepped back, leaving him to Rebecca's mercy. "I needed a change of scenery," he replied briskly.

Another song started while she looked to Peter expectantly. He took a deep breath. He had agreed to dance. "Do you dance, Miss Allen?" He turned his full attention to her, getting his promise over with.

"I enjoy dancing very much," she replied, wistfully.

"Excuse me, Miss Hawthorn. I will return soon." He smiled affectionately. Patience smiled, a new light dancing in her eyes. She was enjoying this act very much. Peter caught a glimpse of something, indignation? in Rebecca's eyes as he talked with Patience.

"Will you check on Miss Gibbon while I dance with Miss Allen?"

"Of course." Patience smiled, moving toward Juliana.

"I don't want to intrude—" Rebecca followed Patience's retreating figure with cat-like eyes.

"We are not yet betrothed. If I had my way, we would be before the season is over. But," he turned his eyes to a surprised Rebecca, "Patience deserves a rest."

He wasn't usually rude, but Rebecca had shown no interest until he attained his father's title. A match with her would be disastrous. Their life together would be miserable for both of them. He wanted what his parents had.

Love and respect.

"Indeed," Rebecca fanned her face. "I had no idea you were courting."

He smiled, offering his arm, leading her onto the dance floor. Her touches and glances lingered longer than was proper, especially with her knowledge of his courtship. "It is a pleasure to see you again, Lord Berkshire." Her earlier reservation disappeared. "I'm so glad you arrived before the season's end."

"I'm happy you are pleased," he said stiffly.

As he caught sight of Juliana, Mr. Westcott by her side, their heads bent, laughing, a protective instinct rose in his breast, and he wished he had not asked Rebecca to dance.

"I did not realize you and Miss Hawthorn were courting."

His attention returned to her. "Yes, I talked with her parents today."

"Haven't you just met?"

"Indeed," he replied, offering no further explanation. She was persistent. Miss Allen's fingers tightened as she took his hand in hers.

"What is it about Patience you find irresistible?" she asked pleasantly, though he could feel her ready to pounce.

Peter, surprised by her questions, took a breath. "There are many admirable qualities about Miss Hawthorn—You should know. She is your friend after all." He paused, trying to come up with a plausible explanation at his sudden attraction to her.

"I see." She paused. "I am not sure if it's my place to tell you that Miss Hawthorn has her heart invested in another gentleman."

Peter's irritation rose. Why did ladies find the need to bring others of their sex down? "Yes, I am aware of Miss Hawthorn's recent heartbreak. We've discussed it at length."

Her eyes narrowed. "I wonder at your affection for Miss Hawthorn when Miss Gibbon is talked of whenever your name is mentioned."

Peter wondered at her interest in him, putting him on

alert. "Yes, well, we are neighbors. We played together as children, and she is like a sister."

Peter found the rest of the dance awkward and stiff, relieved when the music ended. He promptly deposited the lady with her mother.

Patience dutifully waited. "That looked enjoyable."

He did not miss her sarcastic tone. Peter was already weary of this little game. He watched Juliana being escorted onto the dance floor by a young man with dark hair and incredibly long legs.

"Would you care to dance?" he absently asked Patience, watching as Juliana placed her hand on the young man's arm.

"I'd rather have a drink," Patience said.

Juliana joined them shortly, her cheeks flushed.

"I noticed you dancing with Rebecca. Was she sour?" Juliana's eyes danced.

"Moderately. Have you taken a liking to any of your admirers?" He redirected the subject from that insufferable young lady. He was tired of hearing her name.

Juliana smirked. "Only a handful are tolerable with conversing. The rest are as dull as beeswax." Her amusing quips made him laugh. She gave him a conspiratorial smile. "I am so glad you are here." Her eyes caught his. "London seems brighter with you in it."

Peter would have responded, but found the words caught in his throat.

CHAPTER 8

JULIANA LOUNGED in the drawing room of her uncle's townhouse with Patience, a book in her lap. She glanced up at Patience, who quietly worked on her needlepoint.

"How is the *courtship* with Peter?"

"Fine." Patience didn't look up when she answered. Something in her tone didn't seem *fine*.

"But?" Juliana prompted.

Patience set down her needlepoint, turning her head to look out the window. "I miss Walter terribly. I want nothing more than to see him again and ask how he's faring. I hope he hasn't forgotten me already."

Juliana was troubled knowing Patience longed for her past betrothed. She paused briefly, trying to figure a way to help. There had to be some way.

"We must go see him," she finally said.

"It would be improper." Patience whirled her head to Juliana, looking startled.

Juliana closed her book, setting it aside. "You said he is working as a barrister?" she asked quickly, the idea taking shape as she thought on it.

"Yes—," Patience said slowly, narrowing her eyes.

"We'll have Peter find out more information as to where he will be. He can escort us to visit him. If Mr. Longman's love is anything like you've described, he is longing for you as much as you are for him. He would be thrilled to see you."

Patience hesitated. "Perhaps it would only cause more pain. My parents already refused him. What hope do we have?"

"Patience, I am surprised at your lack of faith. I am sure if you are meant to be together, it will happen— money or not. The next step is to let him know you still love him deeply."

Patience's brows knit together, a tortured look marring her features. Juliana wished she could console her friend and make everything turn out right. But she knew what an uphill battle they faced. If her parents would not allow them to wed, the only other option would be to run away with him and face social disgrace. It might ruin Walter's business prospects as well, and he would have nothing to support a wife with.

A nervous smile graced Patience lips. "You are right. I need to tell him how I feel."

Juliana gave her friend a hug. "I'll send a note to Peter then he will help us puzzle it out."

Two hours later, Peter arrived. He stepped into the drawing room, a mischievous smile tugging his lips upward. "I am afraid to know why I am summoned." He took a seat in front of the girls, and reclined back, crossing his legs.

"Do not get too comfortable." Juliana leaned toward him. "We would like you to find out Mr. Longman's whereabouts."

Peter sat up, his eyes bulging in exasperation. "Have you gone mad?"

Juliana stared at him in annoyance. "Why is it lunacy for a woman to want a second chance at finding happiness? Huh, Lord Berkshire?" If she had known he was going to give her such a scolding, she would not have involved him.

Patience rushed in. "If Lord Berkshire thinks it foolish, perhaps we better not try."

Juliana's eyes widened at her friend. "He has no sense of adventure. Besides, he has never been in love. He does not know the pain you suffer."

"And have you, Miss Gibbon?" he asked dryly.

"I have not been in love with a man," she paused, thinking. "I love my ducks that come back to me every year."

He chuckled. "You and that blasted lake!"

She narrowed her eyes. "Someday I hope to be very much in love. I do not think I should marry without it."

He stiffened. "Yes, well, let us hope it does not happen for a good long time."

"And why is that?" she scoffed.

"Because your husband is going to have a very hard time with you. Perhaps if you mature a little more, you will become a woman of sense."

"Peter! How can you be so cruel? To me, and to dear Patience."

He let out an exasperated breath. "I have bent to one of your foolhardy schemes once. I will not do it again."

"Then why don't you take yourself away? Patience and I will put our heads together and figure a way to locate him ourselves."

He stood, pacing the room before standing in front of her, his irritation deepening. "You will not go traipsing about London alone. Promise me."

Patience put her hand over Juliana's, her eyes pleading her to promise.

"You are not the only man whom I can call upon to help. Mr. Westcott has said I only need to send for him to be at my beck and call." She shot that last part at him.

Peter scowled, but the fire dimmed, and she knew he would acquiesce. He let out a long slow breath before responding. "I have read in the paper today that Mr. Longman is working on a high-profile case involving a peer. If we go to the court house, we may get lucky and find him there."

Juliana squealed. "Thank you, Peter."

"Yes, well, we better get to it before I change my mind."

Juliana popped up from her place on the settee, helping her friend up as well. Patience didn't seem as excited about their new adventure, but Juliana knew if they just had a chance to see each other, all would turn out well in the end.

"I will meet you out front in five minutes. If you are not there when I am ready to leave, I will take that as a sign that you have repented of this foolhardy business." He put his top hat on his head before grabbing his cane. When he stepped out of the parlor, Juliana rushed Patience to ready herself. Peter would make good on his promise and leave them behind.

The girls carefully stepped inside the hackney that Peter had ordered. Peter slipped in, taking his seat in front of the girls. They jolted back as the cab took off, clattering down the stony streets.

"Thank you for this, Lord Berkshire," Patience said.

"It is my pleasure." Peter nodded slightly. "I hope we can find your gentleman."

Juliana held in her smile at Peter's answer. His polite veneer had slipped neatly into place. She looked out the window as they moved along London's busy streets. She yearned for her lake, for the thicket behind her home. Her friends from Newbury had made London sound so magical, but Juliana found it quite the opposite. If she hadn't met Patience, or if Peter hadn't come, she doubted she would have lasted this long.

The carriage pulled alongside a stone building, and Juliana stared at the ancient building, the Old Bailey she mused. She had heard of the edifice, but had never been here. "It is much smaller than I expected, being attached to Newgate I thought it would be larger," she wondered aloud.

"Do you think he will be here?" Patience asked coming alongside Juliana while Peter gave instruction to his driver.

"I hope so. We can inquire inside." Juliana took a step in the direction Peter pointed.

Gentleman of various walks of life milled about the entrance.

"This way." Peter gestured up the staircase, but before they could take a step, a voice echoed through the entryway.

"Lord Berkshire, what brings you here with such lovely companions?"

Lord Danbury sauntered up to the group, his eyes sliding toward Juliana. She shifted at his gaze. He'd taken notice of her but she suspected it was the size of her dowry that enticed him.

Peter bowed slightly. "Just giving the ladies a tour.

They had a mind to see where the courts of justice take place."

"I have it in mind to join you. With two stunning young ladies, how can I resist?" He leaned forward, his voice booming loudly through the building. "You may have inherited a title Lord Berkshire, but you mustn't keep both of these lovely ladies to yourself!"

No one laughed at his attempted joke, but Peter allowed a smile to humor the odious man.

"Of course not. Miss Hawthorn, may I?" Peter took Patience's gloved hand and tucked it in his arm. Leaving the baron to escort Juliana.

She wanted to scream. Peter did that on purpose.

"Lord Danbury," Juliana did her best to smile. The scent of tobacco mingled with rancid wax assaulted her nose.

Patience gasped, drawing away from Peter. Juliana turned to see what had startled her. A young gentleman in barrister robes halted on the stairs, eyes on Patience, his mouth parted in surprise. Brown eyes darted from Peter to Patience with betrayal lurking behind them. Without a word, he hurried past toward the entrance.

Patience face flushed pink. "Wait—" she murmured. "Walter, wait!"

Peter grasped her arm before she could flee after him, his countenance remorseful.

Juliana's spirits plummeted as her brain flipped through their options. She had to set this right. It was her fault they were in this predicament. She must tell Walter that what he'd seen had been a lie. She moved forward, forgetting Lord Danbury.

"Miss Gibbon, it would be unwise to enter London's streets unescorted." Peter's voice halted her.

Mr. Longman left the building not even turning at Patience's plea.

Juliana turned to Peter, her heart hammering, her throat dry. Peter's frown deepened, giving her a warning look. He stood rigidly beside Patience, her eyes wide, her hands clasped tightly in front of her.

"I sense something amiss," Lord Danbury said in his booming voice, looking from one to the other, a confused look on his face. "What seems to be the matter with your party, Lord Berkshire?"

"It has been a long day. I believe we will take our leave. Good day, Lord Danbury. I must get my charges home." Peter took Patience's arm, guiding her out of the building while Juliana stood resolute, trying to decide whether she would disregard Peter's decision. Lord Danbury's gleaming eyes took in the length of her body, causing her to rush to catch up with her escort. How had he managed to marry *three* times?

Juliana scanned the street for Mr. Longman, but it seemed he had disappeared.

"What must he think of me?" Patience wailed, turning her attention to Juliana in distress. "I should send him a letter explaining the situation."

Peter turned to Patience. "This is only a slight hiccup. I am sorry I fell for Juliana's scheme. I knew it was a bad idea."

"Did you see the look he gave me?" Patience looked at Peter, not satisfied with his answer. "I don't believe he'll ever forgive me. I've lost him forever."

Juliana's heart plummeted. She'd lost Peter's confidence and injured her friend. She patted Patience's arm, vowing inwardly to set things right.

"Hush now, you have not lost him. We will get you back together with your barrister before the season's up. Isn't that right, Peter?" Juliana looked to Peter, willing him to help her this one last time.

"Miss Gibbon, it is not my place to interfere with the Hawthorn's' wishes." Peter cleared his throat uncomfortably.

Juliana's mouth dropped. "Peter—," she hated it when he called her that. She knew he ment what he said and that was the end of it.

Patience set a hand on Juliana's arm. "He's right Juliana. If my parents found out Lord Berkshire was helping me to see Walter, I'm afraid it would be very bad for him, especially since they think we're courting." She looked at Peter as he opened the carriage door and offered his hand to her. "Thank you for all the help you have been. I believe a letter will help smooth things over until the next time I am able to see Walter."

Peter smiled as he helped Patience into the carriage.

Before helping Juliana inside, he leaned his head close. "Do not interfere unnecessarily, Juliana. I implore you."

"Unlike some people, I go out of my way to help a friend in need," she grumbled. Irritated that he would help no further.

His face darkened, but he kept his mouth closed. She stepped into the carriage, sitting next to her distressed friend. Silence accompanied them home as Peter glared the entire way. The fault was hers, and she must remedy it.

The carriage stopped, and Peter walked Patience to her door. She couldn't hear their conversation. Then he was back.

"I see your mind working. I would advise you let this be, Juliana. We've done enough damage."

The carriage pulled to a stop again a few doors down. Juliana felt her heart jump into her throat as a footman opened the door. She frowned as she fumbled her way out of the carriage, straightening her skirts before stepping to her uncle's door, slipping inside before Peter could help her. She couldn't believe Peter expected her to do nothing. She closed her eyes, a headache growing behind them.

She would set things right.

CHAPTER 9

JULIANA WALKED to Peter's London townhome, her maid in tow. He stood from the armchair where he had been reading when she entered the room. Taking long strides, he met her as she approached.

"What is the matter?" he asked, concern touching his features.

"I need to talk with Mr. Longman about yesterday," she announced. "I have thought all night. It is the only way I see to remedy the problem I have created."

Peter groaned. "Juliana," he pleaded. "You will only make this worse. Let Patience deal with this, it's her life and you must stop interfering. There is no need to besiege the gentleman with more of your schemes."

"But it was all my fault for pushing you into this ridiculous courtship. My fault for encouraging Patience to see him—"

Peter stepped forward, placing his hands on her shoulders. She cast her eyes downward.

"Juliana, look at me."

Lifting her head, she locked on his bright blue eyes. They softened and her heart danced. "None of this is your fault. It was simply a matter of being in the wrong place at the wrong time. It was a circumstantial flaw. There is nothing for you to fix."

She stepped away, dropping onto the settee tucked beside the fireplace. "I am afraid I will not rest until I see him and make this right for Patience. Besides—I want to see if he'd consider making an offer for her again."

Peter sat beside her. "That's folly, Juliana. You'll only make things worse and it's not your business."

"But I feel that it is …"

"Well, it isn't," Peter said firmly. "Promise me you won't contact Mr. Longman about his *past* attachment to Patience."

Juliana remained silent, gazing at the painting hanging above the pianoforte. His mother had painted a tranquil lake with swans swimming amongst flowering lily pads.

"Juliana? Did you hear me?" Peter asked in exasperation.

"Yes," her eyes returned to his.

"But you will not promise?"

"I will not." She stood, and he followed so close she

could feel his warmth. She backed away, not liking the sensation that coursed through her. "I'm sorry to have disturbed you. Good day." She curtsied, spun on her heel, and left Peter, not waiting for a reply.

Ordering her to not meddle only made her more eager to speak with Mr. Longman.

Sarah followed her out to the street. She should have an escort to the Old Bailey, but if she took Sarah, she would tell her uncle, and he might forbid her. Maybe Mr. Westcott would accompany her? But then he'd have to know that Patience and Peter's courtship was ... No, the only way it would remain private was to do this alone.

Juliana walked to her uncle's residence. Feigning a headache, she asked that her supper be brought to her room. Sarah fussed over her, then slipped out, leaving Juliana alone in her bedchamber. Juliana fluffed up her pillows and covered them, tucking her lace cap on top in case her maid checked in later. The maid would think she was sleeping. Donning her spencer, she tucked a few coins into her bag before sneaking downstairs, careful no one spied her.

Safely outside, she walked down the street before hailing a hackney. The driver took her direction before she climbed in, closing the door behind her, she pulled down the sash. Her heart pounded as the conveyance moved forward. Determined to speak with Mr. Longman, she hoped to find him and that he'd listen.

The groom helped Juliana out of the carriage when she arrived. She quickly strode to the entrance of the courthouse, ignoring the surrounding glances. Inside, she found herself out of her depth. She held out her hand to stop an older gentleman as he walked past.

"Excuse me, can you give me the direction of a Mr. Longman?" The man peered down at her, a quizzing glass perched on his eye and a disdainful look on his face. When he didn't answer, she went on, persuading him to her cause. "It is very important that I see him."

The mustached man wrinkled his nose before dropping his spectacle and answering her in a condescending tone.

"I am afraid that's impossible, ma'am. I believe Mr. Longman has left. Some emergency at home."

Juliana's heart deflated. "I see. I am sorry to trouble you."

The man huffed one last time before moving away, emitting a disapproving grunt.

An emergency at home? Juliana walked from the building. Peter was right, she should not have come. Back on the crowded street, she found her hackney had gone. She scanned the street, looking for another. But all that passed were already occupied.

People moved passed, paying little attention. She might walk, but feared she would get lost or accosted along the way. Her fashionable clothing felt conspicuous.

She was out of place, a lady unchaperoned.

A few men gave her odd looks as they passed, perhaps wondering where her companions could be. She knew it was highly irregular for a woman of her class to be wandering London's streets unaccompanied.

Juliana bit her lip, clutching her bag tighter. She lifted her arm, but the hackney rode past. Her chest tightened. She must not lose hope. A fine carriage clapped past, then pulled to a stop. Juliana looked to see Mr. Westcott's head hail from the window.

"Miss Gibbon!" he called. "What are you doing in this part of town? Are you alone?"

"I was just on an errand, but I'm afraid my hackney has left."

Mr. Westcott alighted from his carriage, gesturing inside. "Allow me the honor of escorting you home, Miss Gibbon." He looked very pleased.

Relief flushed through her as she lifted her hand to her throat. "Oh, Mr. Westcott, you are wonderful. I'd given up hope that a hackney would stop." Taking his offered hand, she stepped into his carriage.

He settled into the seat facing her and tapped the roof with his cane.

"It's unsafe for a lady like yourself to be wandering the streets alone. Where was your uncle?"

"Yes, I know," her cheeks grew warm. What could she tell him that wouldn't fall flat?

"I would have been more than happy to offer my

services."

Juliana smiled at his kindness. Had he only known. "Thank you. I should have thought of you. I will remember you in the future." She lowered her voice. "You won't mention finding me alone, will you? I realize it could set tongues wagging."

Mr. Westcott feigned surprised. "Of course, you need not ask. It will be our little secret. I will not tattle." He gave her a conspiratorial smile.

She laughed nervously. He seemed too pleased at catching her alone. She feared she may regret going against Peter's advice. She did not have long to dwell on her misgivings.

They stopped in front of her uncle's home, and Mr. Westcott opened the door, helping her from the carriage. His hand gently squeezed hers while his head ducked down, his lips near her ear. "I wanted to ask you, Miss Gibbon, if I could escort you to the Royal Theater. I have greatly enjoyed your company."

Juliana's insides jumped. "If my uncle agrees." She smiled, giving him a little of what he asked for his gallantry. Mr. Westcott did not find her foolhardy. She wished the thought gave her more pleasure.

Mr. Westcott kissed her hand then let it go, moving back to his carriage. Juliana watched him, fanning her face for fear her flush would raise unwanted questions. She let out a long slow breath then stepped inside, returning to the safety of her room.

CHAPTER 10

PETER HADN'T HEARD from Juliana in days, which wasn't like her. Even though she didn't like the strictures of society, she had never missed an outing. She begged off attending the Opera with them last evening, and he needed to know why. Was she ill? She better be. This entire scheme involving Patience had been her doing. She begged off. He expected her to stand with him.

Had he been too hard on her?

Unless... she wouldn't.

If Juliana had gone to see Walter Longman against his advice…

Peter retrieved his hat and stepped onto the street.

Juliana's uncle lived a few blocks away and the brisk walk settled his temper. It wouldn't do him any good to charge in accusing her. After all, she may have justifiable reasons for deserting him.

The butler answered his knock. "Is Miss Gibbon home?"

"Step this way, my lord."

Peter followed the man to a small parlor where Mrs. Gibbon sat.

"Lord Berkshire, ma'am." The butler retreated.

"Peter, how good to see you." Her cheerful greeting warmed him.

"I've come to visit Juliana if she is well."

"Oh yes, I believe she is in the back gardens. She said something about fresh air," Mrs. Gibbon offered.

"May I join her?"

Mrs. Gibbon nodded, picking up some needlework as she returned to stitching.

He found Juliana sitting on a stone bench, a book in hand. She lifted her head as he approached.

"Peter!" She stood.

Peter admired the red of her dress, the flush in her cheeks, and her attentive eyes. "I was worried. I haven't seen you in days." He stepped closer, brushing his sleeve against her shoulder.

"I'm fine," she returned to the bench, putting distance between them as he sat beside her. "Did you enjoy the Opera?"

"It was boring without you. I missed your company

last evening. You are supposed to help me with this courtship. It was your idea, remember?"

She picked at the spine of her book. "I was——." Her expressive determination gone, he wondered if she'd had an argument with Patience.

"Have you talked with Patience?" he asked cautiously.

Juliana nodded, bringing her eyes to his. He slid a little closer on the bench, loving the warmth of her nearness.

"She's still upset about Mr. Longman. She has not heard from him since sending him a letter."

Peter sighed. "Perhaps he no longer has an interest in Patience."

"That can't be true," Juliana urged. "Maybe he hasn't received it. He may have returned home to the country. Something could have happened to his family."

Peter's eyes narrowed. "Juliana, do you know something?"

She pressed her lips together, lowering her eyes. "I may have heard something to the effect," she said vaguely, admiring the roses to her left.

"Juliana—did you visit Walter Longman after I advised against it?"

"He wasn't there." Fire flashed in her eyes.

"Did your uncle take you?"

Juliana turned away from him.

"Your maid?"

She shook her head.

"You didn't go alone?" he grabbed her shoulders and turned her towards him. "Answer me, Juliana," he spoke more harshly than he should.

"Yes, I went alone," she said defiantly, her scowl searing into him.

His pulse quickened. "How foolish can you be, putting yourself in grave danger?"

"No one knows but Mr. Westcott," she argued. "He promised he would not tell anyone."

A protective instinct reared inside him. "Mr. Westcott?" he snapped.

"Yes!" Her voice rose. "Mr. Westcott happened upon me in the street and offered to escort me home. Which he wouldn't have had to do if you had escorted me like I urged." She turned up a defiant head, stubborn. Just like when they were children.

Peter shot to his feet, anger heating his face. "So, you went behind my back and meddled in this whole Walter Longman situation, anyway. And then rode home *alone* with Westcott? Juliana, if any harm had come to you—."

"None did, thanks to Mr. Westcott, and he was a perfect gentleman," Juliana said coldly as she stood, her book tucked under her arm. "I think he rather likes me. He enjoys my laughter and wit and doesn't trouble himself with ordering me about."

Peter bit his tongue to keep from giving her a verbal

lashing. He ground his teeth. "Perhaps you'd like to marry him then."

"Perhaps," she shot back.

He stepped close to her, so close he could count her lashes. It took all his willpower not to take her in his arms and kiss that ridiculous pride out of her. "You're mingling in high society, Juliana," he warned, his voice low. "Pray, don't make a fool of yourself."

Her eyes glittered with irritation. "You're not my brother," she whispered. "You need not protect me from myself."

He clenched his jaw. "Someone must."

Not waiting for a reply, he turned and stormed through the house, marching out the front door. A stiff drink, that's what he needed and possibly a second. Juliana was driving him to drink.

Juliana couldn't stand it any longer. She and Sarah walked to Patience's townhome, itching to spill her frustrations to someone, someone who would understand. Peter had never behaved so boorish in her presence. He'd scolded her many times, but that was out of respect. This was something different. He still saw her as a child, and one who couldn't take care of herself. If he had his say, she'd probably remain a spinster.

Why hadn't she told him she had attended the

theater with Mr. Westcott that night? She almost did, but then he accused her of backing out of their agreement.

The butler led her to the parlor while Sarah went below stairs for a chat with the staff. Patience greeted her as Juliana collapsed in an armchair. It was a blessing that they were alone.

"Peter Berkshire is the most insufferable gentleman I have ever been acquainted with. He treats me like a child!"

"What did he do?"

Juliana straightened. "He arrived at my uncle's today berating me for trying to plead your case with Walter."

"You spoke with Walter?" Patience's eyes lit with interest.

Juliana felt a pang of guilt. "No... I attempted, but he has returned home to the country."

"Walter's returned to the country?" her friend's voice dropped.

"I believe so."

"Why was Peter so angry?"

"I may have gone alone." Juliana played with her skirt.

"You may have?" Patience shook her head.

"All right, I went alone only because I knew my uncle would forbid it, and Sarah would have tattled."

Patience shook her head again. "It was a rather risky

thing for you to do, Juliana," she said gently. "I would never have asked it of you."

"But I felt so consumed with guilt," Juliana moaned. "I had to make things right. A letter just didn't seem enough."

"Why did you tell Peter?"

Juliana had sworn she would not breathe a word to Peter.

"It just—slipped out," Juliana sighed. "I used to tell Peter everything. He's like an older brother to me. I—I suppose I wanted him to applaud my bravery."

Patience raised her brows. "Brothers don't encourage women to roam London without an escort."

Juliana looked down at her hands. "You're right. I don't know what I was thinking."

"What did Peter say?" Patience asked.

The memory of Peter's words rose in Juliana's mind, and her blood ran hot with irritation. "He called me foolish, alluded to the idea that I needed someone to look after me. He treated me like a child. I felt so humiliated."

Patience folded her hands neatly in her lap. "Have you looked at the situation through Peter's eyes?"

Juliana lifted her eyes to the ceiling. "No. And I don't want to." She didn't want Peter to be right in his chastising, but deep down she knew she was wrong.

"Well, maybe you should try," Patience said calmly.

"Peter did no wrong. He is only concerned because he cares deeply for you."

Juliana laughed out loud. "We have been the closest of friends, but I think he overstepped today—"

"No." Patience shook her head. "You mistake my meaning. I think—" she paused, a hint of a smile touching her lips. "I'm fairly certain that Peter has a romantic attachment to you."

Juliana stiffened, a nervous giggle escaping. "You do not know the two of us. We are friends, that is all. We find joy in each other's company because we grew up together. There are no romantic notions between us. I promise."

Patience laughed outright. "Juliana, I can't believe you are so blind!"

"I refuse to acknowledge the possibility. Even if Peter has these feelings, his affections have changed."

Patience bit her lip. "Are you sure?"

"I'm sure." Juliana took a deep breath, trying to calm the sudden fluttering of her heart. Her throat had suddenly gone dry.

Patience looked down, plucking at the fuzz on her dress. "If you insist. The only reason I went along with this courtship ruse was because I thought it might tease out the romance between you two."

Juliana felt her face heat. "You thought—? Peter and I—? Patience, you have the wildest imagination."

"Doesn't it make you the tiniest bit jealous when

Peter dances with me? That he follows me around at the parties we attend?"

Juliana breathed heavily, internally scolding herself —her tantrums were childish, and she didn't want to give Peter anymore notions that she was a child. "No, certainly not. Besides, I know you don't have feelings for Peter because you love Walter."

Patience smiled. "What if Peter asked for my hand, and I accepted?"

Juliana paused, her heart leaping into her throat. The image of Patience and Peter holding a wedding at the parish in Newbury made her want to throw something. "Then I would be happy to have you as my nearest, dearest neighbor." The warmth that had melded into her words came out brittle.

Patience smiled. "As you say."

Juliana pressed her lips together. "Let us change the subject. I grow weary of talking about Peter. Has Walter answered your letter?"

Patience eyes misted, "No. He has not." The grip around Juliana's chest loosened.

"I am sorry," Juliana reached for her friend's hand.

CHAPTER 11

JULIANA STEPPED in front of the looking glass, admiring her gown. The soft white set her skin aglow, and the embroidered-leaf pattern along the bottom reminded her of home.

Would Peter like it? The thought of her friend caused her heart to ache at how they had last left things. She had felt so independent here in London, but Peter reflecting on her mistakes caused her to second guess. Was Peter right?

Her aunt was joining them for tonight's ball. It was rumored to be the highlight of the season.

She stepped into the carriage, her mind on Peter, understanding now, that she was in the wrong and felt embarrassed at the thought. He was sure to gloat. She took in measured breaths as the carriage came to a stop.

She spotted Patience and Peter when she entered the

grand hall. Patience smiled and waved while Peter watched, not a twitch of a smile on his lips. Juliana waved in return. She was used to his smiling eyes, but it appeared he had not forgiven her yet.

She resolved to take Peter's advice and obey the rules society expected.

Mr. Westcott approached, bowing low. "You look like a dream, Miss Gibbon." He looked with appreciation.

"Thank you." Her polite smile minimized the fact that she was still torturously thinking of what Peter thought of her. "How are you this evening?" she asked absentmindedly.

"Eager to dance. I plan on staying by your side all evening." Mr. Westcott grinned before offering his hand. "May I have this first dance?"

"You may." She followed him as he led her onto the dance floor.

"Have you noticed Miss Rebecca has switched her interests?" Mr. Westcott nodded in the direction to his right.

Juliana followed his gaze to see Rebecca dancing with Lord Danbury. Rebecca chatted easily and pleasantly while Lord Danbury replied loudly. She shuddered at the thought of having to dance with the man.

Did Rebecca really want status and money alone? Or was her mother, who whispered in her ear, pushing her toward the gentleman, no matter their compatibility?

"Besides money, what might Miss Rebecca see in the baron?" Juliana wondered aloud.

"Does it matter? She only cares about his title. Everyone knows her schemes."

"Is there to be no shared affection between her and her future husband?" Juliana asked.

Mr. Westcott's brown eyes searched hers. "Is it affection that you seek, Miss Gibbon?"

"I have a long list of things I'd like in my husband," she said. "But it would surprise me to find a man who fit half those characteristics." Her spirits deflated at the thought.

"Name some of them," Mr. Westcott coaxed.

She studied him curiously. The tender affection in his voice caught her off guard. Mr. Westcott was always in jest. "He should make me laugh every day," she started. "Should genuinely care about others, most especially those who cannot help themselves."

"Like children?" Mr. Westcott asked.

"Yes, like children," Juliana agreed. "He should not mind my singing and playing of the pianoforte at late hours."

Mr. Westcott laughed, and she felt herself relax in his presence. "And he should love me with every fiber of his being, every tremor of his soul." She bit her lip; the conversation had become too intimate.

Mr. Westcott stepped closer than the dance required, his soft eyes caressing her features. "I've had the pleasure in encouraging laughter from you at our every meeting," his voice softened. "I haven't any children, but I would like several. For I am a child at heart. And —," He moved closer still.

Juliana's heart beat hard against her chest as she placed distance between them. "Say no more," she whispered. "The night has only just begun, and there are many other things to talk of."

The fire dimmed in Mr. Westcott's eyes, but it was quickly replaced with his usual mirth. "As you wish." He glanced over at Patience and Peter. "Do you suppose they are quite in love?"

Suddenly, the whole ruse seemed ridiculous. Foolhardy. The room grew smaller, making it difficult to breathe while her thoughts became muddled.

"Certainly not," she spoke before thinking, unable to stomach the idea.

"Is something the matter, Miss Gibbon?" His eyes concerned, as if he knew her thoughts.

She touched a hand to her cheek as she felt her flesh heat. "I think I might need some air. Excuse me." She broke contact and pushed past couples and chatting groups, trying to breathe. Her head pounded. Thoughts of Peter spending his life with Patience agonized her, and she refused to examine why.

She found a side door and exited, pressing herself

against the cool stone of the building. She closed her eyes, breathing deeply, absorbing the night air.

Had Mr. Westcott almost proclaimed his love for her?

She would have refused him. Refused him and ruined the night for the both of them.

Could she marry Mr. Westcott?

Although she liked him, his wasn't the face that surfaced continually in her mind. She clenched and unclenched her fists, trying to clear her thoughts. Peter and Patience didn't have any romantic attachments. Patience was meant for Walter and Peter was meant for — Never mind who Peter was meant for. She shouldn't be concerned.

The problem?

She was!

He constantly filled her thoughts which could mean only one thing. She wasn't prepared for these feelings. All Peter would ever see in her was a little sister who needed constant supervision. She held in a sob as she placed a hand over her mouth, closing her eyes to block out the world. She tried to control her emotions and push Peter back into the place he belonged.

Peter's chest constricted watching Juliana converse with Mr. Westcott. Though he could not hear their conversation, the looks they gave and the unacceptable closeness they shared during the dance revealed their feelings. The thought of Juliana becoming the wife of that man raised the hairs on the back of his neck. To think of Juliana married to another man. The things they would do—twisted his insides. Why was he thinking such things? He shook his head. What would Mr. Gibbon think of him if he could decipher his musings? He turned to find Patience watching him.

"Lord Berkshire, do you even try to hide your affection for her?" Patience asked, a small smile played about her lips.

Peter's eyes moved from Juliana to Patience.

"What do you mean?" Peter stood taller, tugging on his waistcoat.

Her smile grew broader. "I'm of the opinion that you care for Juliana very much — romantically, even."

Peter shook his head, his eyes again searching for Juliana but she had disappeared. "Not at all. We're like siblings." It sounded lame, even to himself.

Patience raised her brows but thankfully did not press the matter.

He spotted Mr. Westcott with a drink in hand, but no Juliana. For a moment, concern took over every other emotion. She had seemed less spirited tonight, more reserved. He feared he'd had a part in that.

He found Juliana returning to the ballroom, standing alone and defiant, her head held high as it often was.

Relief rushed through him. He reverted his attention back to Patience. "I'm sorry about Walter Longman."

Patience looked away. "Perhaps it was not meant to be."

Peter did not know how to respond. His eyes sought Juliana again, feeling uncomfortable with this situation.

Patience groaned beside him. He turned to her, alarmed. "What is it? Is something the matter?"

"You are the matter. You haven't been able to keep your eyes off Juliana all evening."

He sighed. "It's because I'm concerned for her. I was rather harsh to her last time we met, and I worry it's dampened her spirits."

"Well, I've noticed Mr. Westcott does an excellent job of lifting them." Patience eyed the man in question.

"Yes, it seems that he does." Peter felt protectiveness mount inside his chest. "They have been at each other's side all evening."

"I think Mr. Westcott is besotted with our friend."

Peter felt his body stiffen, his nerves on alert. "Do you think she returns his affections?"

Her smile was sly. "It remains to be seen."

She was taunting him as if she was trying to make him jealous. His eyes narrowed. "You are a terrible matchmaker."

Her brows raised, looking slightly offended. "Me? Matchmaker? Never. I am just pointing out what I can see."

"And what do you see?"

She pressed her lips together as a new dance number began. "Let us dance."

Peter gritted his teeth but offered his arm. They entered the floor and took their places. Peter's heart clenched when he noticed Juliana amongst the set.

Patience smiled but said nothing. Thank heavens, Peter didn't feel like initiating it. His mind was too busy formulating his apologies to Juliana. He and Patience switched dance partners.

Two more rotations, and Juliana's soft hands landed in his. "I'm sorry," he blurted and found Juliana's words had echoed his. He smiled, and she giggled, looking away.

"It was unwise of me to do what I did," she said. "I am sorry I caused you some pain."

"I am sorry my words were so harsh," he told her gently. "I had no intention of offending you or dampening your spirits."

Juliana smiled at him. "Friends?"

Peter squeezed her hands, choking out the word, "Friends." He nodded, rotating to a new partner.

After the dance, Peter and Patience came together again. He cleared his throat. "You really think Juliana might—feel more for me than friendship?" The words sounded foreign out loud.

"You should ask her," Patience admonished. "I can see that you feel for her."

He'd always had feelings. It wasn't until arriving in London that he considered she meant more to him than friendship.

"Go. Talk to her. Before Mr. Westcott makes her an offer," Patience whispered.

Peter nodded.

Peter and Patience conversed with many people for the next hour. Peter grew weary of the party. His eyes found Juliana, who was dancing with Mr. Westcott.

He caught her watching, then glanced away.

Somehow, this gave him courage. "Excuse me," he said to Patience. He strode straight toward Juliana, not caring that Mr. Westcott was in the middle of speaking.

"Miss Gibbon, may I have the next dance?"

She straightened, "Yes, I would like that." A light blush touched her cheeks.

Mr. Westcott bowed, taking his leave.

Peter and Juliana stood facing each other, silent. He offered her his hand as the music began. Wordlessly, they joined the rest of the couples on the floor.

"Are you looking forward to returning to Alder Court, Peter?"

His smile broadened at her using his given name. "Yes. You were right in your letter when you said London is dirty and crowded. Besides, I worry for my mother."

"Have you written her?"

"I have, but her letters are brief. I take comfort in knowing she has many friends to keep her company."

"I'm glad to hear it."

They settled into silence, dancing around each other, exchanging hands, and taking careful steps.

"Will you host a party upon your return?" Juliana never took her eyes from him as she asked her questions.

"Certainly not, but my mother will." Peter smiled slightly. His mother, grieving or not, would love to host a party. It was what she lived for.

"I would enjoy that very much," Juliana said.

There was something wrong with their conversation. It was too formal and stiff, nothing like their usual banter.

"You're assuming already that you'll be invited," he teased.

Her mouth dropped open in mock offense, and already he saw her mood lighten. "I will take your lake if you don't invite me."

"You've claimed it as your own already," he reminded her.

"Yes, but you've never acknowledged the fact."

Peter laughed. This felt better, natural. Patience was getting inside his head, making him second guess his feelings for Juliana, though he couldn't deny craving her touch whenever her hands left his.

"Will you go riding with me tomorrow morning?"

Juliana's brows raised. "How? Beast is at home."

"Driving. I meant driving." Juliana was making him tongue tied.

She smiled. "Where will you take me? Hyde Park, at the fashionable hour?"

The thought of having the Ton scrutinize his every move made him second guess his plans.

"No. Let's be daring and go at an unfashionable hour," he teased. "A drive just out of town. I grow tired of the city and would like to stretch my legs."

Juliana brightened. "Can we? Oh Peter, I long to see the country."

"I will ask your uncle and pick you up at ten."

He was rewarded with a radiant smile that didn't waver the rest of the evening.

CHAPTER 12

JULIANA HAD EATEN an early breakfast and was adjusting her straw bonnet. The door creaked and Sarah stepped in, her bonnet and shawl neatly in place.

"Miss Juliana, the Earl is downstairs with your uncle."

"I'm just about ready, I'll meet you in the hall." Juliana picked up the shawl laying across a chair and, with one last look at her reflection, she moved to join her uncle.

Peter had secured permission from him the evening before, and Sarah was excited to join in the outing.

Peter stood in the hall, where her uncle smiled affectionately as she slipped on her gloves. "My dear, you look the image of your mother when she was your age."

"Uncle Henry, you'll make me cry." Juliana lifted on her toes and planted a kiss on each of his cheeks.

"There, there, my dear." Her uncle seemed pleased. "You two young people have a pleasant drive. It will do you good to get out of the city."

Her uncle retreated to his study while Peter offered his arm.

"Where are we going today?" Juliana asked.

"I shall tell you on the way." Peter guided her toward his carriage.

"It can't be a secret," Juliana's brow shot up. It was not like Peter to keep her in suspense. No, that wasn't true. Peter loved to keep her guessing.

"No, but I like to raise the suspense. In case you dislike the place we're going." His teasing smile relaxed her.

"I shall enjoy anywhere you choose as long as you are with me." She did not miss his pleased expression at her answer.

"Let us not suspend our wait any longer."

Peter helped Juliana into her seat while his young groom helped Sarah into the jump seat where a basket lay on the floor, causing very little room for its occupants.

As Peter wound through the city, it did not take long for them to be out of familiar territory for Juliana.

"Can you tell me now where you are taking us?"

He turned to her with a smile before looking back to the street. "I thought you would like to travel north since you have not been this far before."

Juliana lit with excitement. "Do you have a particular destination?" She would trust Peter to take her anywhere but was curious where they would spend the day.

"We are going to Hampstead Heath. It is a bit of a drive, but I have packed us a picnic and there are some ponds I thought would remind you of home." His smile broadened at her excited exclamation.

"Oh Peter, I cannot wait to see it, perhaps there will also be some ducks to remind me of my friends from home."

Peter laughed. "Perhaps."

The ride took the greater part of the hour, but Juliana hardly noticed as Peter kept her occupied with his tales from his past visits to London. He pulled alongside a grove of trees when they'd traveled the park for just a little. They'd traversed a hill, and upon the break, she could see the city of London.

"The view," she breathed in awe.

"I thought you might like it." He hopped from the carriage before helping Juliana alight. "This is the highest point from which to see the city. The heath runs from Hampstead to Highgate and to the north sits Kenwood House, the estate of the 3rd Earl of Mansfield."

His groom was already down, awaiting orders from his master.

"Stay with Miss Gibbon's maid. We will be back in time for lunch."

The footman nodded, and her maid smiled in amusement. Juliana suspected Sarah was happy to stay with the young footman.

Peter took her arm and led her to a fallen tree.

"I do not wish to sit just yet. I would like to stretch."

Peter smiled, standing next to her. "The season is almost over and I confess, I'm looking forward to returning home."

She turned, studying his features and wondering why he had come. "You need not stay. I am sure your mother longs for your company."

"Who would keep you in place?" he teased.

She had to wonder if her father hadn't sent him to watch out for her. It would be just like him. Juliana didn't like the idea. She'd gotten it in her head that *Peter* had chosen to be here with her.

"Mr. Westcott would make sure I did not get into too much trouble."

"Mr. Westcott would lead you headfirst into trouble. The man has no sense, especially when it comes to you."

Juliana wondered at his irritated response.

"He is not as bad as all that. He has much more sense than Lord Danbury." She giggled, thinking on all the times she'd avoided the man's company. "He smells better too."

"Yes, well," Peter grumbled.

"We should try to figure out the mystery."

"What mystery?"

"About why old Lord Danbury smells of candle wax?"

Peter smiled. "He probably counts his money by candlelight."

"I think you've hit on something. He seems interested in large dowries!"

"I am afraid that puts you, my dear Juliana, in his crosshairs."

"I'd rather be trussed and dished up than marry that odious man!"

Peter laughed. "Well put. Fear not, I am sure your Mr. Westcott might save you. Though I'd be careful of him."

"If you are implying he only wants my money, I think not. I am sure he has some excellent prospects besides myself."

"Westcott is a second son. His estate could not continue if his intended doesn't bring money to the marriage. If not, it will force him to work for his living."

"Mr. Westcott has more going for him than you imply. He will make any woman a fine husband." Why was she defending the gentleman? She did not wish to marry Mr. Westcott.

"I would say you'd better stake your claim fast then, but I'm afraid you have already let the whole of society know of your preference for Mr. Westcott. You danced almost all evening."

"I will keep that in mind. He has not yet made an offer, but I am sure it will come. He is not the sort to play with a lady's affections." She marched toward the trees, irritation burning in her chest.

Peter appeared not to be affected by Mr. Westcott's attentions. Has he grown an affection for Patience? The time they spent together had the gossips speculating when an engagement would be announced. Her throat tightened at the thought. She closed her eyes as she wrapped an arm around the trunk of a tree, dispelling the image of Patience in Peter's arms.

A hand touched her shoulder, "I am sorry, Juliana. Whoever you choose will be a fortunate man. If that is Mr. Westcott, I will say ne'er a word against him."

She released slow calming breaths, fearing Patience was wrong. How else could Peter be so calm at the prospect of her wedding another? She kept her eyes closed. Afraid he'd see her pain. "Will you please give me a moment?"

"Of course." Peter's quiet footfalls sounded as he retreated to the overlook.

She would not lose her friend over these feelings. Peter's friendship was too precious. If he preferred Patience, she would be happy for them.

She found Peter laying on the blanket, leaning on his elbow, shuffling a deck of cards.

"Would you like your parasol?" His eyes followed her as she sat down. Laying her bonnet aside, she straightened her skirt, feeling uncomfortable as he watched.

"I suppose I should. But if I am not liked because I have enjoyed a day in the sun, I had best stay clear of that gentleman. For I cannot see myself stopping my habit of walking to my lake unfettered even after marriage."

"You will marry a gentleman who owns a lake then? Or do you plan to stay regularly with your father?" Peter teased, the cards shuffling through his fingers.

"Both, I daresay." She threw her shawl over her shoulders.

"You had better make sure your husband does not object to your trespassing. If I cannot like the gentleman, I do not see myself sharing the lake," his lips twitched.

She scrunched her eyes, taking the deck from his fingers. "Let us settle this once and for all. A game of piquet. If I win, I get full possession of the lake. If you win, the lake is yours."

Peter's smile broadened. "When are you going to learn I will always win against you in sport?"

Juliana lifted her chin. "This is not a sport. This is a lady's game."

"Piquet is no more a lady's game than I am eager to run to Gretna."

"I shall just have to prove you wrong." Juliana finished shuffling the deck and placed it in front of him.

"By all means, try. But I am also fond of my lake and will not give it up easily." He dealt, placing Juliana's cards beside her.

She picked them up, fanning them before her. Placing them in order, giving him a confident smile. Peter might boast, but she held cards that would help her win. She placed the card in front of him with a triumphant smile. The game was on, and she could only guess who would be the victor.

***

Peter sat up, concentrating on his hand. Math came easily to him, but he knew well that Juliana could be a formidable opponent. He could not let her win. He would not mind giving her the lake, but the thought of her sharing it with Mr. Westcott drove him to distraction, no matter how calm he appeared. That lake was a special place because of Juliana. They'd swam there often and confided with each other when they were both still young. She knew his innermost desires and thoughts. No, he would not lose the lake or Juliana to the honorable Westcott.

Peter watched the emotions flicker across Juliana's

face as she concentrated on her cards. What would his life would be like if she became his? There wasn't a soul he knew that wouldn't drop anything to help her. She'd fit into his household like a glove. Her father would be on the adjacent estate, basking in his grandchildren.

Could he win her affections away from Mr. Westcott? He had another side she hadn't seen. The strong, capable man, ready to do whatever it took to make her happy. He was no longer the boy of their youth, full of playful banter. But first, he would win the game.

He placed his card on top of hers and took the winning trick. He watched as her brow furrowed in disappointment.

"Don't worry, I'll allow you to visit the lake *if* you choose your husband wisely." It was too tempting not to tease, just a little.

She huffed before standing and flattening the wrinkles of her dress with her hands. When she brought her eyes back to his, the sorrow in her eyes made him second guess his treatment of her.

He stood, moving to her side. "I promise to stop teasing if you wish. Of course, you will always be welcome at the lake or anywhere else on my property. I would never intentionally offend you."

She looked at the view of the city. "I am not upset about your teasing."

"What is it?" he moved closer.

"My father—" she paused, and he knew instantly her concern. The thought agonized him. But he had to comfort her, even knowing by doing so, he might lose her forever.

"Mr. Westcott's home is in Berkshire, not so far from Newbury and he's not tied to his family home as I am. If he loves you enough, he will live wherever you ask."

"I do not know. Let us talk of other things."

"Are you hungry?"

"I am famished," she smiled, giving him a nod.

"After we eat, I would love to show you the gardens at Kenwood House. They have a wonderful orangery."

"I would love to see the ponds."

He motioned the groom to retrieve the luncheon basket. Juliana kneeled before it and opened the lid. She arranged the dishes and filled his plate with his favorite things, handing it to him before making a plate of her own. His heart filled as he watched her take care of him.

He set the plate down, shrugged out of his coat, and untied his cravat. When he lay on the blanket, his arm propping his head, Juliana held back a smile.

"I thought it was highly improper for a lady to spy on a gentleman in his underclothes."

His lips turned up at her teasing.

"Do not worry, I shall leave the rest of my clothing

on for you—this time." He smiled at the blush that rose to her cheeks.

CHAPTER 13

THEY PACKED the remainder of their lunch and moved back to the carriage, taking the short ride to the ponds. Peter could not get enough of Juliana's excitement at being around water. He imagined she would make a great fish if it was proper for her to swim, though he knew she broke conventions often enough.

They walked to the water's edge. Juliana threw small chunks of bread near the fowl. The ducks quickly surrounded them, clambering to catch their share of the food. He breathed in the clean air, relishing the reminder of home.

"They appreciate the treat, I think." Peter looked at Juliana's profile.

As she turned to him, his breath caught. The sun glittered off her golden curls, making her look as if she'd just dropped from heaven.

"I think so." Her smile turned to him, happiness showing through every feature on her face.

He had a sudden desire to be on the water with her. "There is a little dinghy just over there. Would it interest you to have a paddle on the pond before we head back?"

Juliana looked where he pointed. "Are you sure no one will mind?"

"There is no one here to object." Hopefully, they would not run into anyone they knew from London. Rowing alone on the lake might be construed the wrong way. It could look bad since they thought him to be courting Patience.

"Only if I can row." She skipped toward the little boat.

He trailed behind, watching her excited movements. Funny how such actions had never caused his heart to feel light before. One trip to London, watching how he could easily lose her, had changed his feelings.

Or had they?

She waited for him as she stood by the boat. He took her hand, steadying her as she stepped in. She sat as he pushed off, jumping in as the boat glided into the water. He sat quickly, taking the oars and slicing them through the water.

"You promised I could try my had at the oars." She leaned forward, placing her hand over his.

He chuckled, relenting to her wishes. She took over

the rowing, slowly pulling as they drifted toward the middle of the lake.

"I better not let you row us back or we will not make it home before nightfall." His smile broadened at her scowl.

"Just sit back and enjoy the scenery." Her smile brightened, showing him she enjoyed his teasing.

He moved to the bottom of the boat, resting his back on the flat board of the seat.

"What are you doing?" She giggled.

"I am sitting back to enjoy the scenery."

"I did not mean for you to take my words literally."

He rested his legs next to hers, challenging her to put him in his place. She just grinned, bringing the oars back into the boat and matching his position. He let out a laugh as she turned her face to the sun, sighing in contentment.

"I could live like this forever," she closed her eyes and inhaled. "It smells of home."

He placed his hand on her legs, relishing the closeness. She didn't seem to mind as her eyes remained closed. He sat watching, waiting for her to stir while her chest slowly rose and fell in shallow puffs. Had she fallen asleep?

"Juliana?" he prompted, waiting for her acknowledgement. She did not wake, and he realized the late night before, mixed with her steady rowing, had probably tired her out.

Contentment washed over him, watching her restful state. She was a vision. His heart swelled, doing laps in his chest as he watched her sleep. If only this could be their reality. He would give anything to make that happen.

The boat drifted toward the shore. The wind not fast enough to make much headway. Sarah and the groom were probably wondering where they were, but he didn't care. He doubted the image of Juliana resting like this would ever leave his mind. He'd treasure it for a long time, even if she preferred Mr. Westcott.

The sun moved to the western sky. It hadn't fallen yet but would soon, given its position. He gently sat up, touching a golden curl resting on Juliana's lovely cheek. It did not wake her, so he lightly stroked her cheek, relishing the softness of her skin. She leaned into his hand as a small smile played on her lips. She did not open her eyes, and it took everything in him not to lean in to give her a kiss. Instead, he took her cheek, fanning his fingers to touch the outline of her jaw.

Her eyes flew open, and she sat up straight in startled surprise, almost knocking him back. She grabbed his shirt in an attempt at steadying him. When she realized her mistake, she quickly dropped her hands, turning to stare at the water before bringing her wide eyes back to him.

"I fell asleep, didn't I?"

His smile stretched. "I would have let you continue,

but I fear we are already late. Your uncle might call out a search party if we do not return soon."

"I'm sorry, I do not know what came over me." She touched the curl that clung to her face, tucking it back in place.

"My early morning call, mixed with dancing all night, I daresay."

"Yes, well. Please don't mention this to anyone. Especially my uncle. I am afraid I have already caused enough trouble." Her nose scrunched.

"It shall be our secret." He rowed the boat, 'til it slid back onto the shore. He stretched his legs, removing the kinks from sitting in the same position.

Juliana sat, brushing the wrinkles from her skirt and he slid the oars into place and stepped from the boat, pulling it clear of the water.

He took her hand, helping Juliana from the boat, and moved to the waiting carriage. The groom rested on a rock, engrossed in conversation with Sarah.

"I'm sorry for the late hour. We lost track of time," Peter apologized.

The groom stood and nodded. "We didn't notice the time passing my lord."

Peter smiled at the cheeky smile his groom gave to Juliana's maid.

They were on their way home in no time, and Peter found he wished the day never had to end.

"We had better get home before dark, or you will

have caught yourself a title," Peter teased. His smile dropped at her nervous glance.

"I hope we can make it." A hint of worry in her voice.

"I'll have you home in plenty of time."

"Good." She scanned the scenery, letting the conversation lag.

He wished to show her how much he cared. But her nervous glances caused him to second guess his plan to capture her heart. He could not read her, and he longed for their banter-filled teasing they shared back home. Had London changed them both? If so, it wasn't for the better. He needed an alternative plan, one that started with breaking off his fake courtship with Patience. The thought of showing his affections for Juliana caused a warm feeling to settle in his heart.

CHAPTER 14

JULIANA WAS TOO RESTLESS to sit still. She'd never had a more wonderful day in her life though her emotions swung from one extreme to the other. At times, Peter did not seem indifferent to her as she once thought. At others, he was convinced Mr. Westcott and she would marry. She had been mulling it over in her mind all day and it had gotten her nowhere.

She wandered the back garden, had been on several walks around the square with her aunt, and even picked up a copy of Romeo and Juliet to occupy her mind. None of it worked. Peter still entered her thoughts at every moment. She replayed the last ball they'd attended repeatedly in her mind. The way his hands seemed warmer, more tender in hers. The way his eyes caught and held hers. The slight press of his palm against her waist as they danced.

It did not help that she'd been caught sleeping in his presence. Though waking up to Peter's hand tenderly brushing her cheek had been worth the embarrassment.

Mr. Westcott could no longer hold her attention. He was soon becoming a memory.

The selfish part of her thrilled at keeping Peter to herself in Newbury. The scheme with Patience had helped bring them together. Still, several young women attempted to catch Peter's attention.

Her aunt swept into the room, Patience trailing behind, interrupting her thoughts.

"Your friend is here to see you, dear."

Juliana's copy of Shakespeare slid to the floor as Patience entered, instantly aware of pain in her friend's eyes. Something was wrong.

Her friend affixed a polite smile upon her face. "Thank you, Mrs. Gibbon." The gracious smile disappeared as soon as Juliana's aunt left the room. Rushing to her side, Patience pulled out a letter, pushing it into Juliana's hands. "A letter came."

Juliana looked at the crumpled note, unease settling in the pit of her stomach. "From Walter?"

"He signs it, but he has such an odd request. It makes me anxious. I do not know what I should do." She squeezed Juliana's hand, crushing the letter further. "Please, read it and tell me your thoughts."

Juliana unfolded it slowly, scanning its contents. Her heart jumped as she read.

.   .   .

My dearest Patience,

I must apologize for my behavior as of late. I would like to explain myself, but there are more urgent matters at hand.

I've recently become aware that you and Lord Berkshire are engaged to be married. For which I wish you the utmost happiness. But I am afraid he may be in grave danger. I am working on a case involving him, the details of which I cannot disclose in this letter.

It is of the utmost importance that I speak with you privately. Please consider meeting me tonight at The Nightingale, a pub in the east end of London. I will be there waiting just before dusk.

This meeting requires the most urgent of secrecies. If you require an escort, ensure that they will not expect to be a part of our conversation.

I cannot stress the importance of the information I must share with you. I expect to see you tonight.

Diligently yours,

Walter Longman

Juliana's throat constricted, her breath hitching. She read the letter again, absorbing its content. She raised her eyes to meet with Patience's.

"Whatever could it mean?" Patience's voice came out in a high-pitched whisper.

"I am not sure." Juliana's hand shook as she handed the letter back. Fear shooting through her at the danger Peter might be in at this very moment, even. "But I am eager to hear what Walter has to say."

"What could endanger Lord Berkshire?" Patience looked confused. "And why doesn't Walter reach out to him directly?"

Juliana frowned. "Perhaps he feels it would be an impertinence of some sort."

"And asking a young woman to meet him at a pub in the east end is not?" Patience prompted, the pain in her voice clear.

It was a strange request. No young lady in her right mind would venture to the east end alone. Juliana had heard the horror of peddlers and prostitutes roaming the streets.

Patience began pacing the room. "I love Walter, and I worry about Peter, but this is too much to ask. I should ask my father to come along, at the very least—"

Juliana shook her head. "Your father would never agree to take you to the east end. No man in his right mind would."

"Then why is Walter requesting I meet him there?" Patience wrung her hands. "He would not ask this; he could not ask this—unless—it is very serious. Walter is a kind, thoughtful man. He would never put me in harm's way. Never." Her voice cracked, undercutting the boldness of her words.

"Perhaps the east end is not as bad as people say," Juliana said, not believing her own words.

"Why couldn't he just ask me to meet him here, where it's safe and proper?" Patience's voice spiked in volume.

Juliana grasped her friend's hands, moving her to the settee, trying to calm her fears. "He knows you are brave. He trusts you. I will be your escort, but whatever he has to say to you, he must say it in my presence. I will not leave your side."

Patience's hand fluttered to her chest, then rubbed against her throat. "I don't like this, Juliana."

"Do you love Walter?" Juliana hoped she was doing the right thing.

"Yes, of course, I do," her lips pressed together.

"And you trust him?"

Her friend's green eyes met hers, and the fear in them ebbed away. "Yes."

"Then we have no reason to doubt him." Juliana shuddered, imagining her and Patience venturing to the east end alone. Patience might trust Walter, but Juliana barely knew him. She cleared her throat. "Perhaps we should bring Peter along—"

"The letter said—"

"Yes, but Peter should hear if he is in danger, do you not think? And I'd feel much safer if he were with us."

Patience nodded, biting her lip. "Yes. I suppose Walter can't expect to send such heavy news and me arrive without Lord Berkshire."

Juliana stood. "Let's go to Peter now."

It was already afternoon. They had little time to convince Peter to come along. As they neared his townhome, Juliana realized he would never let them come with him. If he went, he'd go alone. She didn't share that thought with Patience, who was eager to see Walter, even in these unsavory circumstances.

Peter was absent, he'd stepped out, the butler informed them. This concerned Juliana more than wandering the east end alone. What if he was already harmed? Bleeding to death in a dark alley? Kidnapped and held for ransom? A protectiveness surged over her as her imagination ran wild. If anyone harmed her Peter, she did not know what she would do. Her stomach plummeted.

Patience watched Juliana, both of them standing in the entry of Peter's townhouse, the butler waiting.

"What should we do?"

Juliana clenched her teeth. "Can we leave a message?" she asked the butler. "It is very important."

"Yes, of course," he gestured with a brief nod. "Come this way."

Moments later they were in Peter's library, where Juliana scrawled a quick note.

. . .

Peter,

Patience has received some upsetting news from Walter Longman. He has requested her presence for a private audience at The Nightingale, a pub on the east end tonight at dusk. Yes, we understand it is dangerous, but we are highly concerned about the information he is eager to share with us. You were not here to escort us, and it cannot wait.

It worries us that Mr. Longman's news concerns you. He has informed us you could be in grave danger. Watch yourself and tread carefully. Patience and I will return shortly after nightfall.

Yours,

Juliana

She folded the letter, entrusting it to the housekeeper who had scurried into the room to replace the butler. "Be sure Lord Berkshire gets this as soon as possible, please." She hoped the housekeeper could sense the urgency in her voice.

"Don't you mind. I assure you he will receive it as soon as he steps foot through the door."

Juliana exchanged a glance with Patience. "Are you ready?" Juliana was already thinking better of their plan, but Peter was in danger. She must be courageous.

"Let's just pay Walter a quick visit." Patience's voice held a note of insecurity.

As the girls exited the townhome, Juliana hailed a hackney.

They stepped inside, ordering the driver to take them to The Nightingale.

His brow wrinkled. "You sure you be wanting to go into that slum?" The driver took in their fine clothing, a skeptical expression marring his face. "'Tis not safe for any Lady, especially ones unaccompanied."

"We are sure." Juliana handed him a Guinea.

The cab driver widened his eyes but hopped on the carriage without a further word, moving the horses forward.

The girls sat silently on the drive over. Patience wringing her hands, and Juliana continuously swallowing to wet her dry throat. As she glanced out the window, she forced her beating heart to slow.

It couldn't be too bad. As long as they stayed in the public areas, no one would dare touch them. She had survived a visit to the courts. But that had been in broad daylight in the west end.

"Something still bothers me about the letter." Patience interrupted her thoughts.

Juliana turned to stare at Patience. Her unease caused Juliana's heart to sink.

"Walter said he'd heard of an engagement between Lord Berkshire and me. He wished us happiness. Did he not receive my letter explaining that we weren't actually

—" she trailed off, bunching the fabric of her dress in her fists. "He must think me terrible."

Juliana took Patience's hand in hers, squeezing her clammy palm. "Perhaps he did not receive it?" Now that Patience had brought up the concern, she wondered as well. Maybe he did not care for Patience as much as everyone believed. Why mention the relationship at all if not out of spite?

The streets became more crammed with buildings, and the streets narrowed, clogged with carriages and wagons. People loitered in the streets, wrapped in rags. She took in the smudges on their ruddy faces. The sun had begun to set, casting deep shadows in alleyways. Men and women alike leaned suspiciously against stone walls, watching the people go by. One woman leered at her as the carriage rumbled past.

Juliana shuddered, but they were nearly there. They could not turn back now. They'd go in, uncover Walter's disturbing news, and leave straight away. If Walter was a gentleman, he would escort them back home, especially as it would be after sundown. The thought did little to comfort her as they slowly weaved further into the gutters of London.

Juliana's mind turned over scenarios for Peter's plight. Perhaps he was in debt to some notorious swindler? Maybe there was a plot to kidnap him for his money? They all seemed wildly inaccurate, fantastical. She burned to know what secrets Walter held.

The carriage rocked as the driver pulled to a halt. He opened the door, squinting at them skeptically.

"You ladies sure this is where you want to be?" His Cockney accent seeped through each syllable he uttered. "Mighty rough part of town, in'nit?"

Juliana's stomach cramped. "Yes, we are sure." She put on a brave face. "We are meeting a friend."

"Ah," the driver sneered, helping them down from the carriage and waggling his brows suggestively. "You're meeting a friend? 'Tis, not my business what a lady does in the night."

Patience reddened, but Juliana's temper flared. "We're no light-skirts," she snapped.

Juliana tipped the driver with a copper token, irritated at his suggestion. "Would you please wait around for a half hour at least? This shouldn't take long."

The driver tipped his hat. "You be most generous, mum. I'll wait around a bit."

"Thank you."

Taking Patience's arm, they turned to face The Nightingale, a tiny pub crammed between two buildings, crouching darkly in the shadows. Juliana couldn't imagine why Walter had wanted to meet Patience here. She was beginning to question her friend's choice in gentlemen.

A dark thought entered Juliana's mind, so twisted that it lodged in her brain, unable to banish it away.

What if this were punishment for Patience choosing another man?

Juliana knew it was ridiculous. The man Patience loved couldn't be that mean spirited, especially when he knew he was far inferior in status and wealth compared to other men in Patience's company. *Maybe that was the problem.*

Taking a deep breath, Juliana led Patience to the entrance of The Nightingale and walked through. The scent of whiskey and gin assaulted their senses. Raucous laughter shattered Juliana's ears, making it hard to focus. Her eyes swept the small pub. She caught sight of a woman, her bodice dipped low, revealing her wears while she handed a drink to a man who grinned at her like a pastry treat in the bakery window.

Juliana looked away in disgust. "Do you see him?" she asked eagerly, wanting this over as soon as possible.

"No." Patience's grip had tightened on Juliana's arm, constricting the blood flow.

A short woman approached them, hands on her hips. "Can I help you, ladies?" Her scowl deepened as she studied their attire.

"We're looking for a Mr. Walter Longman," Juliana explained, hoping this woman would have some answers.

The woman snorted. "Never heard of 'im." She looked the girls up and down. "Methinks you lot are far from home." She waved her hand, dismissing them. "Out with ya. We want no trouble here."

Juliana and Patience exchanged glances. "He's not here?" Patience's voice twisted in disappointment. "I don't understand. Why would he—"

A hand snaked along Juliana's waist, pulling her to a dark figure. She pushed back, gasping as panic set in. A man covered in filth ogled her. "Come to make some quid, my pets?" he asked through rotting teeth.

The bar maid swatted him with a towel. "Back off, Tully. These ain't your girls."

"We should be going." Juliana backed away. "Sorry for taking up your time."

The woman only snorted, turning back to her work.

Juliana and Patience hurried out of the cramped pub, moving into the street. Tully followed close behind. Patience whimpered, moving closer to Juliana's side.

"I don't like that man," Juliana hissed as she scanned the streets. "He smells of trouble." The hackney was nowhere in sight.

Panic raked at her chest, constricting her throat. Her palms broke into a sweat.

Tully shoved himself between them, wrapping arms around their shoulders.

"You'll fit right in with my girls." His sneer deepened into a lustful look. "I have many customers who would be mighty pleased. Mighty pleased, indeed."

Juliana swatted him away. "Don't you lay a finger on us again." She tried to sound outraged.

Tully's grin only grew. "Be a good girl now."

His hand locked around Juliana's wrist, letting go of Patience altogether.

A scream ripped from her throat, but a hand grabbed Tully's front, pulling her out of his grasp. Juliana watched in horror as a fist smashed into his nose. Tully stumbled back with a filthy curse.

Juliana rounded on their rescuer, her eyes landing on Peter. His blue eyes were ablaze like never before as fury darkened his features. They snapped to Juliana, making her heartbeat quicken.

"Are you harmed?" His voice was low and furious.

She shook her head mutely as the fear ebbed away, replaced with despondency. Patience whimpered at her back, clutching her arm.

Peter turned his focus back on Tully, tightening his fists. He bent, hauling Tully upright, and hit him again across the jaw. "Crawl back to the hellhole you spawned from." Fire raged in his dark eyes. Juliana thought he might kill the man.

Tully moaned, clambering to his feet. His nose bleeding profusely. With another curse, he jogged away, disappearing down the dark alley.

"Peter," Juliana breathed with relief.

"Is he here?" Peter asked, the anger not yet

dissipated. "Walter Longman?" he asked again when no answer came.

"No." Patience quietly stepped in.

An ache settled inside Juliana's chest as she took in Peter's disheartened expression. He could barely look at her. Peter set his jaw, twisting at Patience's words. "There was foul play here tonight. Make haste—I cannot stand the stench of the place."

He led them to the carriage he must have hailed soon after receiving her note. He helped them inside, averting eye contact with Juliana. A slight tremor shook his hands as he rushed them inside. She'd never seen him so angry. He would never forgive her for this.

"I'm so sorry, Peter." Patience broke down, trembling, her hands twisting her dress until it was a crumpled mess. "Walter would never put me in harm's way. Walter wouldn't—"

"If that man is indeed responsible for tonight, he will pay dearly." Peter's voice was low as his gaze fell on Juliana. She squirmed, finding no warmth in the glare. "What were you thinking, Juliana? Marching into the east end unaccompanied at dusk? I thought you'd know better."

Still shaken from their encounter with Tully, tears pricked at her eyes. "I was worried about you," she flung back. "The letter said—"

"Hang the letter," Peter growled. "You always do this! You fantasize about saving the day without giving a thought for yourself. It will be your ruin. My ruin—" he trailed off, taking his fingers to the bridge of his nose, calming his breaths.

Juliana clamped her mouth shut and turned to the window. He was right. She knew he was, though the thought brought little comfort. She'd just irrevocably damaged her relationship with him. His reaction to their safety solidified the knowledge that he was forming an attachment to her friend. Peter wasn't finished.

"Both of your reputations could have been destroyed tonight. Or worse. What do you think that low life had in mind for the two of you? I don't care what the bait is — promise me you'll never set foot on the London's streets without a proper escort, Juliana."

She bit at her tongue, frustrated with herself. Frustrated that Peter had to chastise her yet again.

"Juliana." Peter's voice was a low warning.

She forced herself to look at him, although heated shame crept up her neck as she said the words he wished to hear. "I promise."

Peter looked to Patience. "Do you have the letter you received?"

Shaking, Patience retrieved the letter and handed it over to him. He scanned its contents. "Deplorable," his voice sliced through the thick tension. "I will have a word with Mr. Longman first thing tomorrow."

"Please do not be hard on him," Patience pleaded.

Peter scowled. "He has put you in danger. He must be dealt with properly."

The rest of the ride was endured in silence.

The carriage stopped outside Patience townhome. She gave Juliana a tight hug.

"I'm so sorry," she choked.

"You have nothing to be sorry for. I encouraged you, as always. I make a very poor friend."

"No," Patience drew away. "You are one of the best friends I have ever had." She offered Juliana a shaky smile before turning, letting Peter help her out of the carriage.

He walked Patience to her door, taking her hand in his and leaning into her as he mouthed something Juliana could not hear. Peter bent and kissed Patience's hand. Juliana closed her eyes as tears squeezed out, falling onto her ruined dress. She was going to fall to pieces, something she never indulged in, especially with an audience. So she pulled her control in when Peter returned, hauling himself inside. She opened her eyes when the carriage jolted forward. She sucked in ragged breaths when her eyes fell on his.

Peter sighed heavily, swiping a hand down his face. "Juliana, I'm sorry. I was too hard on you."

She held out a hand. "Stop!" She drew out her words carefully. "I deserved every word. I am a fool. I doubt I'll ever return to London again for all the trouble I've caused."

Juliana's disgrace deepened when he didn't respond. Losing Peter would be hard enough. Knowing the shame he felt over her was worse, but she would not let him pity her. She bit her lip, holding back tears that burned behind her eyes. The shock of the recent events, the fear and confusion, they all crashed on her. She held her breath, longing for solitude so she could release the tension with a cleansing cry.

"I wanted to kill that man back there," Peter mumbled.

Juliana kept her gaze fixed on the window, knowing that if she looked at Peter, she would lose the control she fought for.

Peter reached for her hand, and she was proud that she didn't flinch away. He held it in both hands, continuing.

"I came as fast as I could when I received your note. I was so worried—Juliana, I thought the worst. I thought I had lost you."

She clenched her jaw. She would not cry. Peter did not let go of her hand until they reached her uncle's. He helped her down from the carriage, and she was careful not to look him in the eyes.

"May I walk you to the door?" Peter asked gently.

Her heart constricted, wanting this evening to be over. "You may," she rasped.

He cradled her hand in the crook of his arm, guiding her to her uncle's home. The polite veneer he added was bitter, catching in her throat. When they reached the steps, Juliana fixed her gaze on the ground.

"Thank you." She strained to say the words. "I don't know what we would have done if you hadn't come."

From the corner of her eye, she watched him clench his fists. "It was lucky you left me the note."

She nodded absently. "Good night, Peter."

She turned to hurry inside, but he caught her by the arm, giving her pause. She turned back, still not meeting his gaze. He gently lifted her chin, forcing her to look at him. His familiar warmth had replaced his anger.

"Please forgive me if I have offended you. I am glad you are safe—Juliana."

He took her hand in his and bent, gently pressing his lips to the back of it, lingering longer than acceptable. Heat rose to her cheeks, her heart fluttering wildly in her chest.

He straightened and bowed. "Good night."

She watched him walk away until her vision blurred. She quickly entered the house, closing the door behind her. She leaned her back against it, against the outside world. Closing her eyes, she could feel herself slipping. Not wanting her aunt to see her out of control, she ascended the stairs and slipped into her room. Blissfully Sarah was not there. She let the tears fall unabated.

CHAPTER 15

PETER CAUGHT the first carriage to Lincoln's Inn, rage quietly twisting inside his gut the whole way there. Thank heavens he found out where Mr. Longman was staying after Juliana had roped him into spying on the man.

Juliana, his heart still shuddered at what may have happened to her and Patience if she had not left that note. And it was luck that he returned early from the club. She had looked so repentant when he left her last evening. It was all he could do not to wrap her in his arms and kiss those pouting sweet lips. He exhaled the thought. Leaving her was the second most difficult thing he had done. The first was agreeing to this confounded courtship. He knew it would only bring him trouble, and it had.

Peter was going to get to the bottom of what

transpired last night and why. Either Walter Longman had been spiteful, dimwitted, or was being used for ulterior motives. What those motives could be, Peter hadn't a clue. Perhaps Walter had offended someone who wanted to harm him indirectly by causing harm to the woman he loved.

It was a mystery, which Peter was determined to unravel.

He strode through the entrance, not stopping as he passed young bucks who looked just out of University. He turned down the hall filled with offices, scanning each door for a plaque that read the barrister's name.

He found it shortly, the wooden plaque tacked to the oak door. Peter rapped at it loudly, hoping it came across as authoritative. He waited, listening, and was satisfied when he heard the scrape of a chair and footsteps padding to the door.

It opened, and Peter found himself face-to-face with a gentleman who blinked in surprise.

"Can I help you?"

"That remains to be seen," Peter growled, watching the other man's eyebrows draw together.

"Do come in," The gentleman offered, pulling the door wide and stepping aside. Peter strode through the door, entering the office, taking in the small space. A little desk covered in stacks of parchment was placed under a window so small, Peter wondered why anyone bothered to put it there at all.

"Please, take a seat." The barrister gestured to a chair. His voice calm, soothing though still guarded. It didn't mean he was innocent.

Peter took the offered chair and waited while the gentleman sat behind his desk, clasping his hands in front of him. A long, handsome face with chiseled cheekbones and a full mouth waited. His dark brown eyes watched Peter cautiously, curiously.

"What can I help you with? I am very busy today. You best make it quick," he finally spoke.

"Are you Walter Longman?"

A light seemed to go off in his eyes. His countenance changed to anger before being tucked behind a wall of indifference.

Interesting.

"Patience Hawthorn received a letter from you yesterday," Peter started, unable to banish the edge in his voice. "Do you deny you sent her a letter?"

Walter frowned. "I do deny it. I've not talked to that lady for a while. Since—" He stopped mid-sentence, his brow furrowing. "Miss Patience's fickle heart can no longer bother me. If you are here because you think I am trying to win back her affections, rest assured. I have banished Miss Patience from my heart." His icy tone caused Peter's hairs to prickle.

Peter pulled the letter from his waistcoat pocket. Opening it, he slid it across the desk. "You requested her to meet you at the east end to speak with her.

About a case you were working. A case that concerns me."

He shook his head, his frown deepening. "You are mistaken," he looked at the letter.

Peter tapped his finger on the parchment. "Have a look yourself. I have proof. You cannot deny it."

Walter looked at the letter again, his icy stare turning to concern as he snatched it up, scanning its contents, his eyes widening. They darted back to Peter. "Did she go?" he demanded. "To the east end? Is she alright?"

Peter narrowed his eyes suspiciously at Mr. Longman. He seemed genuinely concerned, but was it an act?

"She did go to the appointment, but I arrived in time. I fear what would have happened had I not. She'll be alright."

Mr. Longman let go of a shaky breath as he glanced at the letter. His hand trembled.

"I did not write this," his voice lowered. "It is not even my handwriting, look." He reached for a stack of parchment, shoving it toward Peter. "These are all correspondence I've written in the past month. Go ahead, compare the writing."

Peter reached for the stack, taking a cursory glance. He clenched his jaw. The handwriting was decidedly sloppier, nothing like that of the letter.

"And look." Walter drew a fresh piece of parchment from his desk, dipping a pen in ink. "I'll write for you now." As he scribbled words, Peter could already tell the handwriting was different.

The barrister handed the newly written words to Peter. He glanced at the sentence. *You can't tell me I've written that letter. I would never put Patience in harm's way. No matter the pain she's caused to my heart.*

"I believe you." Relieved Patience's love wasn't psychotic. He took the letter, folding it into his pocket again. "But who did? Do you know anyone that would hurt her?"

The barrister's features darkened. "I can't imagine anyone wanting to harm Miss Patience. What could have been the motive?" He winced as if someone had slapped him. "Goodness—she believes I sent that letter. She thinks I put her in harm's way. She thinks—"

"I will explain our findings to her," Peter promised. He stood. "I need to get to the bottom of this. You have no idea who could have written this?"

Mr. Longman shook his head, also standing. "None."

Peter sighed. "If you think of anything useful, reach out to me immediately."

"Perhaps the letter was intended to harm you and not Miss Patience. Your intentions to her have been written in all the gossip columns," he scowled.

Peter's eyes widened. Shock rushing through him. Walter was right. This letter was intended to harm *him!*

And the culprit nearly succeeded. If he'd lost Juliana, he would have never recovered.

"I will inform you if I have any news. Thank you for your help. I think you might have hit upon something." Peter turned to leave, stepping out of the office before turning back to Mr. Longman again. "Patience still—"

"I thank you for giving me this information. I shall do my best to uncover the mystery, but I have a mountain of work ahead of me and cannot waste my time on something that no longer concerns me. Good day." He shut the door, ending any further communication.

So, he had received none of Patience's letters. His hard reserve hadn't fooled Peter. He still loved Patience, yet could not forgive her for not going through with a wedding. Peter could understand, but he still deserved to hear the truth from Patience. Peter could not blame the man. He knew the torture of knowing the woman he loved was intended for another. It was time. He must release himself from their scheme so he could find out for himself where Juliana's heart truly lay.

CHAPTER 16

PETER WOULD TELL Patience what he had learned of the letter, and her parents had to be informed that Patience would withdraw from this courtship. He wasn't looking forward to the latter for both their sakes. He knew given her mother's reaction she would not let him bow out easily. He suddenly wondered why he had let himself get tangled up in this mess.

He was graciously welcomed into their home. Mrs. Hawthorn tripped over herself trying to make him comfortable, depositing him in the sitting room and fetching Patience. Peter stood awkwardly as he waited for Patience. Her father sat in a comfortable-looking chair by the hearth.

Peter cleared his throat when Patience entered, her arm entwined with her mother's, who looked as if she was ready to sing joyous accolades to the happy couple.

He shifted uncomfortably. His eyes darting from Patience, who eyed him eagerly, and then to her mother.

"I wondered if—perhaps, it was possible that I speak with Miss Patience privately?" Peter knew this sentence alone would get their hopes up. He tried not to give anything away in his expression.

Mrs. Hawthorn's eyes grew to the size of saucers.

"Of course." She gripped her husband's elbow, pulling him from his armchair. "Come along, dear."

The father did not appear as excited as his wife, though he obeyed easily enough.

Peter watched as they left the room, closing the door behind them. It would disappoint them that there would be no wedding. He stepped to Patience as the door clicked behind them.

"It was not Mr. Longman who sent the letter," Peter reassured her.

"How do you know?" She placed her hands on his, her eyes still anxious.

"I just came from his office."

Patience stepped back, catching her breath. "You questioned him? Did you tell him of our farce?"

"No, I'm afraid he would not let me speak of you."

"He still thinks I have changed my affection to you?" She fell onto the settee, her eyes misting.

"I don't think he has received your letters. Though he gave enough of his feelings away for me to know that he still cares deeply for you. He was relieved you are safe and wishes me to tell you he would never intentionally put you in harm's way."

Patience nodded. "We must put an end to this game. I think it best we stay away from each other. The gossip will settle when we are no longer seen together."

Peter nodded. "I agree." He sat next to Patience. "I am sorry things went this far. I should have never agreed to this. But it made me realize something."

Patience looked to him. "What?"

"I love Juliana."

Patience shot from her seat. Her mouth dropped open. For a moment Peter thought she might jump up and down in her excitement. "I knew you loved her!"

Peter smiled at her sudden change in mood, thankful her spirits were back.

"I have no idea how she feels. Do you suppose she could love me back?"

The door to the sitting room opened with a bang. Mrs. Hawthorn marched through.

"In love with another?" she asked with a shrill cry. "Lord Berkshire, you've become attached to someone other than our daughter?" The incredulity in her voice made his heart plummet into his stomach.

Patience deflated beside him.

He should have suspected Mrs. Hawthorn would eavesdrop at the door. He cleared his throat, though he knew nothing could change the awkwardness of this situation. But he must try to save what was left of his dignity. His mouth opened.

Patience's voice rang with defiance. "Mother, Peter and I were never attached. We set this up so he and I could enjoy some peace, so that you would stop pushing gentlemen my way. Peter loves Miss Gibbon, and I love Walter Longman. Nothing you can say will change that!"

"I don't care who loves whom," Mrs. Hawthorn snapped.

Mr. Hawthorn peeked his head inside the room, watching the rising conflict.

Patience's mother puffed herself up. "Lord Berkshire asked if he could court you, and I consider it a breach of contract that he wishes to offer for another without consulting us."

"Mother, I never had any intention of marrying Lord Berkshire." Patience drew herself up to her full height. "If he had made me an offer, I would have refused it."

Mrs. Hawthorn huffed. "And I would have forced it upon you! Now close your mouth, I don't need any more explanations from you. I want to hear Lord Berkshire come to his own defense."

Patience glared at her mother, and Mr. Hawthorn looked to Peter as if he were an actor in a show. Peter squirmed. He was not at all prepared to handle the situation.

"Mrs. Hawthorn, I had no intention of offending

you. Please forgive me. I understand now that our scheme was insensitive. I'm sorry for toying with your feelings. I am deeply sorry that I have harmed your trust in me."

Mrs. Hawthorn scowled at him. "This is unacceptable. I demand that you wait until we get this situation settled before speaking to Miss Gibbon."

"Mother, stop it," Patience snapped. "You are being ridiculous."

"*I'm* being ridiculous?" Mrs. Hawthorn turned to her husband in disbelief. Mr. Hawthorn remained emotionless, watching the drama unfold from the door. "Mr. Hawthorn, tell Lord Berkshire he must stand by his offer. Demand it of him."

Mr. Hawthorn's eyes flicked to Peter's. Conflict boiled behind his eyes—the fear of refusing his wife and the fear of making a confrontation with an earl. Peter felt sympathy for the man.

Mr. Hawthorn shuffled heavily from one foot to the other before moving into the room.

"Lord Berkshire," he paused, clearing his throat. "We are very disappointed that you agreed to this foolhardy endeavor, causing my wife great pain. However," he said with a hesitant glance at his wife, "it is not my place to demand anything of you. Just know that you have lost our trust, and we no longer consider you a respectable man."

Mrs. Hawthorn's chest blossomed red, but she did

not argue with her husband. She turned her glare on Peter.

"I understand," Peter said with a bow. "I hope to one day regain your respect and trust. I am deeply sorry. To show how much I value you and your daughter, I extend the offer for you to stay at Alder Court whenever you like for however long. You will be most welcome."

Mrs. Hawthorn did not seem satisfied with his answer, but Mr. Hawthorn nodded.

"Thank you," Mrs. Hawthorn said through tight lips. She gestured toward the door. "Now, if you will excuse us, we will leave for home tomorrow. Patience, we're ending your season now."

Patience's eyes widened. "Mother, you can't!"

"Yes, I can," she snapped. "Get your things together. I don't know why you're so insistent on Walter Longman, but we will not permit you to see him again!"

Tears welled up in Patience's eyes.

He longed to comfort her, but there was little he could say or do. It was out of his hands now.

He bowed to Mrs. Hawthorn. "Forgive me," he muttered before leaving. His heart suddenly heavy.

CHAPTER 17

JULIANA MADE HERSELF SCARCE, hiding away in her bedroom, claiming illness. Reading until she thought she would go mad. She could not concentrate on the words. Every time she tried, an image of that foul man would pop into her mind. If Peter had not saved them, she would be unreachable from anyone of good society. She did not even want to consider what that would have done to her father. He was right to have denied her London for so long.

Now, Peter would tell him of her shame, and it would ruin her in his eyes. She had already lost Peter, and she thought her heart would break. She would witness his happiness whilst her own would happiness would be lost forever.

She threw Shakespeare aside. Romeo and Juliet's

love was a tragedy, and so was her life. But at least they went together to their grave. She stared up, counting the rose petals on her canopy. Her uncle had not called her down, which meant he did not know of her escapade yet. There was nothing for her to do but to take courage and go to her aunt.

She ventured out of her room, quietly poking her head into the drawing room. It lay empty, so she slipped in, sitting in a large winged-back chair. After five minutes of solitude, she jumped up and moved to the back sunroom facing a small garden where her easel sat. Painting would keep her mind occupied. It worked for Peter's mother, though Juliana's painting was paltry compared to the new dowager's, but it did the trick.

She added a lopsided boat to her river she'd already painted and wondered how Patience fared. She must be as miserable as she, knowing Walter might have sent her to such a place. She could not bring herself to believe it was from him.

She dipped her brush into some water, splashing it around to clear the paint, then placed it onto a towel to try. Just as she was about to find her aunt, the door opened, and Peter marched outside. Juliana stepped back, her mouth dropping in surprise.

"Peter!" She didn't know what to make of his sudden appearance. Her throat went dry. This was a miserable way to greet her friend.

He stood awkwardly by the door, not answering her exclamation. He clutched his hat, his back stiff. Her heart sank. She did not know this awkward Peter. She opened her mouth to try to salvage what was left of their relationship, only to be interrupted.

"I cannot banish you from my mind," he said in a rush, moving closer to her. "After the events of the other evening—Juliana, how are you faring?"

She moved back at his declaration, not knowing what to make of it. She pressed her lips together.

"Well enough, I suppose. How is Patience? I have not been a diligent friend."

He averted his eyes, noticing her easel.

"Are you painting?" His familiar smile touched his lips.

Juliana set her hands protectively on top of the small canvas. "I beg you not to look. Your mother would be ashamed."

A glint lit in Peter's eyes. "Well, now I'm curious."

"Peter—"

Not heeding her protests, he walked around to stand beside her, his eyes taking in the river meandering across the canvas. He nodded, his smile stretching in the silence. Was he judging her poor attempt at painting?

"Hmm. Clever use of color here." He pointed to some red roses that didn't belong on a riverbank.

Juliana shook her head, biting her inner cheek. She

looked at him, deflated. She couldn't even paint properly. "The water looks as if it's boiling."

Peter laughed. She shifted, eventually settling into an awkward silence.

Juliana sensed tension coming off him in droves. She shifted awkwardly again, finally sitting down.

"Would you like to sit?"

He obliged, taking the armchair across from her. He cleared his throat, leaning forward, elbows on his knees.

"Mr. Walter Longman did not write the letter," he blurted. "I checked with him. The handwriting is noticeably different. I am convinced he didn't write the note to Patience."

Juliana's eyes widened. "Then who?"

"I'm working on discovering that."

"How did he take the news that Patience is not courting you?"

His eyes locked on hers, and she gulped at the sadness she saw there.

"He doesn't know. He wouldn't give me the chance to explain. Though he will find out soon enough."

Her heart dropped for her friend. "Does she know yet?"

"Yes, I just came from her residence. And, I, well —" He could not seem to get the words out, and Juliana's heart throbbed. They will force him to marry Patience. Had his affections turned to her? —Juliana could hardly bear the thought.

"Has Patience caught your affection? Is that why you are unable to tell me the rest of your news?" Juliana forced a smile, even as her heart was breaking. She deserved every bit of it, and Patience deserved to be happy. Peter would make any woman a wonderful husband.

Peter shifted in his seat. She'd never seen him so agitated.

"No." Peter cleared his throat. "I mean to say—I am afraid our scheme did not turn out as well as we hoped. Patience is being forced to return to the country. Her mother's determined to keep her from Mr. Longman. I am afraid we will not be seeing her for a while."

Juliana frowned, gulping back the lump that had lodged in her throat.

"This is all my fault," she whispered. Peter did not deny her statement. "Is there anything we can do to fix any of this?"

He narrowed his eyes. "Juliana, please get it out of your head to try to fix your messes. It is too late for all of that. Anything you do will only make matters worse."

She nodded. "You are right. I have learned my lesson. I just wish I had an excuse to run back to the country."

"I am returning as soon as I can close up my townhouse. If I could take you with me, I would. But I'm afraid that would only cause more gossip. Besides, you have your Mr. Westcott to cheer you. But before I go—" His eyes locked with hers, seeming to look into her soul. "Juliana. Is there anything I can do? Anything you need?"

Juliana blinked in surprise, then squared her shoulders. He was *not* her Mr. Westcott.

"You act as if I'm suffering an illness."

He clapped his hands. Leaning forward, his eyes focused on her lips. It did strange things to her heart. Slowly, she leaned toward him. He was terribly handsome. No wonder the ladies felt a need to apply their fans when he was about. She wished for just a small kiss before he was lost to her.

"Tell me something," he said, leveling his gorgeous blue-eyed stare. "How involved are you with Mr. Westcott? Really and truly, I mean. Has he captured your heart?"

She pulled back as if someone had dumped cold water, turning her to ice. She hadn't expected that.

Determined to be honest, she gulped. "I believe he nearly made an offer at the last ball."

"Ah." Peter looked away. "And—would you have accepted?"

Juliana faltered. "I—I don't know." She couldn't let Peter know her genuine feelings. It was clear he wished to pawn her off on another. He was done with her and all the trouble she caused. Could she blame him? She caused him nothing but frustration since he'd been in London.

Peter was back on his feet. He clutched at his hat, twisting it in his fingers.

"Juliana—you must know. You must have some inclination about my feelings for you."

Her lips parted, stunned at his words. She felt her heart thud against her breast. Could he possibly?

He pressed on. "I've always viewed you as a little sister. But—I cannot stop thinking of you. Your laugh makes my heart race. I long to be near you. I—I love—" He stopped. "But—if your feelings aren't aligned with mine, I understand. Westcott will make a fine husband if that is who you want."

Juliana couldn't tear her gaze from Peter as the enormity of what he'd just said sank in. Her heart lightened, and a giddy sensation replaced her sorrow. The lump still clung in her throat, but she forced it down as she tried to control her emotions. She covered her mouth to stop a happy outburst, but the giggles escaped, oozing between her fingers.

Peter frowned, cocking his head.

"Are you laughing at me?" His eyes narrowed in exasperation, frustration lurking behind his eyes.

She shook her head, removing her hands. "I do not want Mr. Westcott." She had to choke out the words. She stood, stepping closer, so close she could see the specks of blue green in his eyes.

Peter's lips parted, but he uttered not a word. His eyes intent on hers.

She took a deep breath. "I may not have realized it when I came to London." Her words slow and deliberate. "But my heart belongs to you. It always has."

Peter let out a long-held breath, stepping closer, leaving little room between them. She caught the scent of peppermint. He had not changed. She gulped, not knowing what to do next.

"Will you be my wife? I want to love and cherish you always." His words were but a whisper.

A tear slipped from her eye. "Peter," she breathed. "Nothing would give me greater pleasure." She leaned in, tilting her lips to his.

He cleared his throat, backing away slightly.

Confused. Had she just imagined the conversation? She looked at the floor.

"Juliana." He took her hand, stroking its top with his thumb. "I need to ask for permission from your father first."

Her eyes joined Peter's, a full smile stretching across her face.

"Since when have I ever stood on conventions?" She pulled her hand from his, twisting one arm around his neck, the other fanning through his perfect hair. She pulled his face toward hers, their lips inches apart.

His eyes shined for a brief moment before a smile appeared. He closed what little space was left, meeting her lips with his. Commanding attention, possessing hers with a fierceness she had not expected. His arms encircled her waist, pulling her flush against him. It felt right. Her heart thudded in her chest, but not in pain as she would have expected but with sheer pleasure, dancing in blissful rhythm.

Peter groaned, clenching his fists at her back, pulling away slowly. She moved with him, capturing his lips again, not wanting the moment to end. Sparks flew even as he fought the pull of her lips. He took what she offered with one last flame. He wove a hand into her curls, grabbing the back of her head and pulling her further into his embrace, just as he had the day of his father's death. Only this time, her heart leaped with joy instead of sorrow. Peter wrenched away, putting some much-needed space between them. He closed his eyes as he rested one hand on the mantel.

Peter's breathing slowed as he fought to gain control. Once he could no longer hear the beat of his heart thrumming through his head, he opened his eyes. Juliana stood before him, her eyes wide in concern. Her lips plump from his kiss. He held her arms, keeping his distance.

He gave her a weak smile. "You need to fix your hair before your uncle sees you. He'll know what we've been doing."

Juliana fingers went to her hair, catching the tendrils

that had escaped at his passionate touch. She tucked them back in place as much as she could.

This was all on him. He should have given her a gentle kiss and been on his way. But even before their lips touched, he knew that would not be possible. He had been wanting Juliana for too long while knowing she would never be his. As realization hit that her heart was his, well, it had not been the best combination to keep his will in check.

"How do I look?"

"Like an angel."

Her face broke into a smile that could chase away every gloomy thought, and she moved into his embrace. He wrapped his arm around her waist as warmth enveloped him like a summer's rain. She didn't try to kiss him again, but her closeness had the same effect. His heart leaped, while he backed away, taking her hand, he led her back to the sofa. Her eyes waiting expectantly.

"I think I will stay in London after all, I need to find out who sent Patience that letter. It is obvious they intended her harm."

Juliana's brows narrowed. "Who could have wanted to harm her?"

"I don't know. But I shall think of something. I worry that you could be in danger as well."

Juliana looked confused. "It was Patience who was in danger, and she is safely on her way home."

Peter shook his head. "I think the letter might have been to injure me. If someone thought I was courting Patience, what better way to hurt me than to take away the woman I love?" His eyes darkened. "If they had succeeded, they would have truly hit their mark. For if any harm came to you, I do not know what I would do."

Juliana placed her hand to his cheek. "You came just in time. And I have faith that you will find the culprit."

"I hope you are right."

She smiled. "Are you going to Lady Wellington's ball tomorrow?"

"How can I miss it when you will be there?" He squeezed her hand.

"I expect to dance with you and keep you by my side."

"Do you think that is a good idea? I shouldn't want anyone to know of our engagement until we find who wrote that letter."

"A few place words and we might flush them out." A twinkle lit her eyes.

"Do not give me that look. You'll be back in the thick of things, and I will not risk you again." He worried she would be the next target.

"I will not be foolish, I promise. Now you must tell my uncle of our plans." She stood, taking Peter's hands, forcing him to stand.

Peter's grin widened as he stooped and stole a quick kiss. "If you insist, my love." He caught her other hand

and guided her out of the sitting room in search of her uncle. Being with Juliana was so natural. He wondered why he'd fought his attraction. He intended to keep her by his side until he made her his wife.

CHAPTER 18

PETER RODE back to Newbury to ask Mr. Gibbon for Juliana's hand. Her father was thrilled and wished Juliana home to prepare. Peter had advised against it because he still needed to get to the bottom of the letter. He'd sent inquiries to no avail. The thought that Juliana might still be in danger because of it drove him out of his mind. They would soon have no choice but to go home and let things happen if anything would come of it. Juliana would be his in less than a month. He'd have a better opportunity to ensure her safety with her by his side.

The banns would be read next week at their parish church where his father was buried. It gave Peter comfort to know that his father would be so close for his wedding.

She'd spent the last two weeks preparing for the wedding, buying her trousseau in town. Word had spread fast about their engagement, and many people congratulated them.

The last ball of the season was grand—everybody who was anybody was there in their finest gowns and pinned-up hair. Juliana's aunt hosted the night's event in honor of her niece.

Peter proudly displayed Juliana on his arm, convinced he had the most beautiful and charming woman in the room.

But there was a sorrow shared between them. It was true, Patience had been taken to her home in Wallingford. Peter couldn't imagine the heartbreak she felt and knew Juliana was blaming herself. It wasn't true, of course, but the ball wasn't the same without Patience here.

Peter watched Mr. Westcott, who was attempting to avoid them. Peter wished him well, just not with Juliana.

"May I offer my congratulations?" Miss Rebecca curtsied graciously before them, her polite smile fettered the irritation behind her eyes. "I must admit, I did not see this coming. I was under the impression Miss Patience Hawthorn had captured your interests, Lord Berkshire."

Peter pursed his lips. "Just a minor diversion," he paused. "Of Juliana's creation."

Rebecca's eyes widened as she turned to Juliana, whose smile only brightened. She was enjoying her moment of triumph.

"There was never an interest between either party," she confirmed with a nod. "Peter was so set upon by unwanted attentions so soon after his father's death, that we thought it a good idea to protect him from it."

"Well." Rebecca fanned herself awkwardly. "That is highly unusual."

"It did not work, and I can't say I am upset about it." Juliana gave him a conspiratorial grin, and he had to work hard at not smiling with her.

Rebecca curtsied again. "May your life be filled with the utmost happiness, Miss Gibbon." Rebecca walked away, finding her partner for the next dance, looking the opposite of what she'd just proclaimed.

Peter turned to Juliana. "Shall we?" his brows raised

"Most certainly." Juliana tucked her arm in his as he led her onto the dance floor.

"Rebecca was cordial with you, though I can see what you meant when you said society only *seems* polite. I never noticed before."

"Yes, that is because there was nothing *seemingly* when it came to you. They were truly happy to have you in their acquaintance." She smiled, and he was again utterly happy that she had chosen him. "She and I have not been on the best of terms. But I suppose she knows when to quit the field."

Peter groaned with a smile. "I don't enjoy being made into a lady's sport."

Juliana just laughed, a pleasant sound.

The dance made it impossible to converse any further.

The music ended, and Peter led Juliana to a group of ladies. As tonight's hostess, she was expected to make everyone feel welcome. She did it with ease. Some girls who had snubbed her before seemed genuinely friendly. Becoming his betrothed had already raised her status. She fit well into his world.

Peter wandered the room, leaving Juliana to bask in her new found attention when Lord Danbury approached.

"Well done, young man." Lord Danbury clapped him on the back. "You've snagged one of the most sought-after young ladies this season."

"Juliana and I have been friends for quite some time." Peter wondered why he suddenly felt the need to justify himself. The gentleman had shown interest in Juliana, but he knew the baron never stood a chance.

"I believe I may make an offer myself before the night is up." Lord Danbury lowered his usually loud voice.

"Oh?" Peter forced down a smile.

"Yes." The baron pulled a letter from his breast pocket. "Lady Allen and I have kept up a vigorous correspondence, and I believe I've formed an attachment to her daughter." He opened the letter, handing it to Peter proudly. "Shortly after you announced your engagement, she gave me permission to court Miss Rebecca."

This man was the most unconventional baron he ever had the misfortune to know. The oddity of the situation was stifled when Peter examined the letter. He froze, his blood running cold.

The handwriting was nearly identical to the letter Patience had received. His heart thrummed against his chest. Lord Danbury was saying something, but Peter wasn't paying attention. He didn't even read the letter, only focused on the way the "I"s slanted and the "d"s curled with shocking familiarity.

"I say, you look a bit peaky, Lord Berkshire. Are you feeling ill?" Lord Danbury's brows rose.

Peter lifted the letter to the baron, his hand shaking. "Do you mind if I keep this letter for a while?" He didn't wait for Lord Danbury to respond, just tucked the letter into his breast pocket before moving away from the man.

He pushed through the throngs of people, scanning for one face. He peered over heads and glanced at occupied chairs.

Finally, in a separate room with French doors splayed wide open, he found her.

He approached Lady Allen, allowing her a stiff bow. "Lady Allen?"

She halted mid-sentence and looked him up and down in contempt. "Lord Berkshire," she rose slowly. "I believe congratulations are in order."

Anger coursed through Peter, but he pushed it down before responding. He needed to get this woman alone so he could keep Juliana's reputation intact.

"Will you please accompany me onto the terrace? There is something I wish to show you."

Everyone around them watched. He shifted uncomfortably. Would he be able to conceal this from society's prying eyes? Lady Allen stood and moved stiffly to the terrace. He ignored the whispers and followed the woman. She moved to the banister and laid her hands upon the cold stone.

"You wrote the letter, didn't you?" His rage was barely concealed, but he didn't care.

Lady Allen blinked, but her teeth clenched. "Excuse me?"

"Walter Longman supposedly penned the letter. He didn't. You sent it. You persuaded Miss Patience Hawthorn to risk herself and reputation by going to the east end. You cannot deny it. Your handwriting is exactly that of the letter."

Lady Allen no longer smiled. Her face had gone pale, and she fanned herself, looking out into the gardens. "Goodness, I have no idea what you are going on about, Lord Berkshire." Her voice had risen an octave.

Rebecca appeared, looking surprised to see him speaking to her mother. "What's all this about?" She looked between them, dropping her normal decorum.

Peter wondered if Rebecca had been in on it, too. "Did you know?" he demanded. "Did you know that your mother forged a letter from Walter Longman and misled Miss Patience, putting her in harm's way?"

Rebecca's lips parted, and she looked to her mother, confusion setting in her eyes. "I don't understand."

Curious faces watched from inside the house. He didn't care that they had drawn attention. He would find out tonight and settle this. Peter extracted the baron's letter from his waistcoat pocket, handing it to Rebecca. "A letter was sent to Miss Patience, calling her urgently to the east end of London. She was almost accosted, and had I not rescued her, she would have been lost to everyone who loves her. The letter was penned in Lady Allen's writing. I can produce it as proof if need be."

"No," Lady Allen snapped. "Rebecca, do not take that letter."

But Rebecca had already reached for it, curiosity overruling her mother's command.

She scanned the letter. Her hands shook. She swallowed, looking up at her mother.

"Mother, you have corresponded with Lord Danbury about my marrying him?" Her voice hitched. Peter could not believe it surprised her, given the attention she had given the man. She shoved the letter to her mother, but Lady Allen backed away. "Everything makes sense now."

Lady Allen thrust her chin up proudly. "Rebecca, whatever you may think, I did it for you. Everything I do is for you."

"But what you have done is cruel!"

Now the attentions of the room were fully on Lady Allen.

"Hush now," Lady Allen snapped at her daughter. "We will discuss this later."

Juliana had moved onto the terrace, slipping her hand into Peter's. The gesture gave him strength. They would overcome this together as a couple. No one would tear them apart again.

"Is it true that you soiled Miss Hannah's reputation last year?" Rebecca demanded, "I thought it below you, but this—" She folded the letter up, her movements stiff. "This proves to me you don't really care for me. You only care for the wealth I might marry into." She scowled. "And I will not marry Lord Danbury!"

She shoved the letter back at Peter, then spun into the house, pushing past the stunned audience.

Lady Allen moved back into the room, taking a shaky seat, looking to the gentlemen and ladies who surrounded her, mouths hanging open. She glanced back at Peter who had followed her in, hatred in her eyes.

"You've ruined any relationship I had with my daughter, Lord Berkshire." The venom in her voice rose.

Juliana pulled him from Lady Allen's view while her aunt started requesting the band to resume. It had hushed once the last dance had ended, everyone having taken their attention to the spectacle.

Juliana took his hand and pulled him into the library.

"I've ruined your party." All the fight had left him, replaced by weariness.

She shook her head, placing her hand to his cheek. "It is our party, and you have ruined nothing."

He let out a long breath before grasping her hand and kissing the back. "I am sorry for my outburst. I could not contain myself when I found that Lady Allen had written that letter."

"We can now start our life together without any more worry. It might not have been the best place to figure things out, but now we can focus on being utterly happy. Who cares what society might think of us?"

"I am afraid I have ruined any chance at being respectable. Society's lips will wag for many years to come."

"I care not for society. All that matters is you."

He pulled her to him, stealing a kiss. He did not realize how much it had affected him until he found the identity of the letter writer. He let the worry slip from him as he concentrated on Juliana's soft lips. She obliged him by wrapping her arms around his neck and pulling him closer. This new Juliana would need further exploring, and he was more than willing to start now, never stopping until they were old and gray.

CHAPTER 19

JULIANA RETURNED home to Newbury with the scandal in her wake. Society would not be forgiving to them for a long while yet. Juliana could not bring herself to care overly much. She only wanted Patience to tell Walter of the mix-up. She did not wish to distress Patience over the discovery Peter had made, but knew she had to know. To think they were in the company of such a woman—and that Juliana herself had put Patience in harm's way by convincing her to pretend to court Peter! She couldn't bear the thought.

As soon as she reached home, she would write Patience a lengthy letter, detailing what Peter discerned and her own profuse apologies. She hoped her friend could forgive her.

Juliana's father was thrilled to have her back home. He greeted her on the drive after the carriage pulled up to her father's grand estate. She jumped from the carriage almost before the wheels had come to a stop, flying into her father's arms.

"What was the point of the season if you would only wed the man down the road?" he grunted and pulled her close.

Her aunt alighted the carriage with her husband's help, a reproachful look on her face. Juliana just smiled at her aunt. Juliana had been an utter failure in London. She did not know why her aunt kept trying to make her respectable. Peter did not mind who she was.

Juliana laughed. "I did not realize it before I left for London, Father. But this season was necessary for me."

Her father patted her hand. "Well, I can't complain. You'll be close by. This is the best agreement that could have ever been arranged." His proud eyes took in the length of her body. She was glad to be home. She could imagine marrying no one else. It would have killed her father to lose her. Now he did not have to.

Peter had followed on horseback, continuing home as her carriage pulled into her drive. She'd only been home a second, and she already wanted to see him. She did not know how she would survive the week without Peter by her side. He would dine with them tonight. Then attend to business until the wedding.

As they moved inside, Juliana took in her home. The season lasted longer than she'd imagined, and she was grateful to be home again. The decorations had not changed. The light yellow of the paper-hangings and the detailed white wainscoting bordering the walls in flourishes gave her a sense of peace. She'd missed the familiar halls of her youth.

"After you wash up from your journey, meet me in the drawing room. I have something to show you before Peter and his family come this evening," her father said.

She untied the ribbon on her bonnet and kissed his cheek before handing her traveling things to the manservant, who stepped into the hall behind them.

"I will not be too long." She moved up the stairs and into her room where her maid was waiting for her. Her maid pulled Juliana's dress off and helped her into a fresh gown of light muslin.

"My sister had her fifth child. She had asked if I could help with the little ones while she rests," Sarah said. "If I am being honest, I am happy to be back. I enjoy taking care of hair more than small children."

Juliana laughed, sitting in front of her mirror. "Well, I am afraid you have your work cut out for you. My hair always becomes unruly once I take off my bonnet."

Her maid smiled as she took out the small pins that held her hair together. Juliana dipped her hand in the fresh decanter of water that was in front of her while her maid worked to fix her hair. Once she was clean, Sarah put the finishing touches on her light chignon. Juliana was ready in no time, eager to spend more time with her father. The maid stepped back, moving out of Juliana's way.

"Go help your sister, I shall be fine until you return. I understand now, more than ever, the importance of taking care of your family. You will have a place with me as long as you like."

Her maid gave her a light curtsy and a wide smile. "Thank you."

Juliana rushed down the stairs, remembering to slow down as she entered the drawing room. Her father sat in front of the fire, a wooden box sitting on the small table before him. She sat facing him, her eyes falling on the out-of-place object.

"Did you find some interesting shaped leaves while I was away?"

Her father's gruff laugh made her smile. "No, I wanted to give you a wedding gift from your mother." He picked up the box and opened it toward Juliana.

A delicate necklace of tiny diamonds in the shape of leaves stared back at her. A matching set of small earring studs sat near the top of the velvet-encased box.

Juliana gasped. The portrait that hung on the wall in this room donned this very set. It was why she loved the lake so. Her mother was sitting by the bank, looking into the water. It was comically unnatural, her mother sitting by the water wearing the expensive necklace and beautiful gown, but Juliana loved the portrait just the same.

Tears filled her eyes as she lightly touched the stones. "Mother's necklace," she breathed, hardly believing what she was seeing.

"Your mother always intended you to have it, just as her mother before her."

Juliana smiled, bringing her eyes back to her father's. Moisture hung in his eyes. "Thank you," she said reverently.

Her father took the necklace from the case, holding it up to her. She turned around so he could clasp it around her neck, then moved to the small mirror and exchanged her earrings out. She stared at her reflection, touching the stones. Her mother's reflection stared back at her. She bit her bottom lip, stopping a cry before turning back to him. No wonder her father loved her so. She was an exact copy of her mother. She'd heard it often enough, but until now had never seen the resemblance so acutely. Her father smiled, drying his eyes in time for her aunt and uncle's entrance.

"I am famished. What has cook prepared this evening?" She stopped, laying her eyes on the shimmering necklace. "You look just like your mother." Her aunt moved to Juliana, taking her hands as she kissed her cheek, forgetting about her hunger. "Though it is a bit formal for an unmarried young lady."

Her uncle sat next to the fire, his smile catching. "She has all but joined our ranks, my dear. Do not fuss."

As if on cue, Peter stepped into the room. His eyes

softened as they landed on her necklace. He knew the importance of her wearing it and moved to her, placing a kiss on her cheek.

"You are breathtaking. I cannot wait until I have you all to myself," he whispered into her ear.

She swatted his lapel. Her face heated. "You will never have me all to yourself. We will visit my father every day."

The room laughed, and she turned her attention to her family.

Peter's mother stepped in, giving Juliana another kiss. "Welcome to the family. I am sorry I could not be with you while you shopped for your wedding attire, but I am planning a large ball to be held in your honor as soon as you return from your wedding trip."

"Mother, that was a surprise." Peter's eyes went wide.

His mother just smiled, her eyes dancing.

The butler announced dinner, and Peter tucked her arm into his. Her father offered for Peter's mother's arm, surprising Juliana, escorting her into dinner. Juliana smiled at the intimate picture they created. She could get used to keeping their evenings small.

Peter turned to her as dessert was placed before them.

"Are you sure you must leave for the week?" she asked.

"It will fly by. I am sure my mother will keep you busy enough that you will hardly notice my absence."

"Imagine if you had not followed me to London."

"It would not have taken me long to discover my feelings. You are looking radiant. I would have noticed, no matter where we ended the summer. Besides, it was the thought of you being set upon by so many admirers that had me scurrying to London. I was jealous, even if I only realized it after."

"I was always so jealous of you heading to London without me. Especially when I came of age, and father still would not let me go."

Peter looked ashamed. "I have a confession to make." Juliana wasn't sure if she wanted to know. "I am the one who convinced your father to delay your coming out."

Her mouth popped open before she remembered her manners. She pursed her lips together, calming herself. This felt like a betrayal somehow.

"Why?" she questioned, pushing back the lump in her throat.

He touched her face gently, stroking the edge of her jaw. She looked to her family, but they didn't seem to notice their closeness.

"If I could take it back, I would. Just to erase the hurt behind your eyes. I promise never to cause you pain again."

She gulped, pulling his hand from her face. "That is

not a promise you can keep. We are like brother and sister, and siblings do quarrel."

"It has been some time since I considered you as a sister, my dear," he smiled.

She pushed back her smile. He always won an argument. "You are stalling. I might have to go back to addressing you as Lord Berkshire."

"I suppose it is fitting. You can call me by my formal title when you are cross with me whilst I shall try to chase away your anger."

This was a lopsided bargain. Peter would always succeed in coming out the victor.

He turned serious. "I noticed your father seemed agitated whenever my father would bring up your going to London. I knew you would be snatched up as soon as you entered society. I suppose I was prolonging your time with him for both your sakes. Maybe even then, I was jealous of my competition." He smiled lazily at her.

She took her eyes to the ceiling. A definite original Juliana trait, as Peter always pointed out.

"I will forgive you if you hurry back to me."

He took her hand to his lips before turning to his dessert. "That, I can promise."

Juliana turned her attention to her father. "How was your summer? I did not write as often as I should have."

"Long." Her father dipped his spoon into the jellied fruit, taking his first bite.

"Do not worry yourself over him. I kept his spirits up while you were away," Peter's mother interjected.

The evening finished in the same jovial manner. Her family let her be alone while Peter said his goodbye. She leaned her head on his chest as he pulled her to him. "Mother will keep you busy. She has been orchestrating the bedroom changes ever since she found out of our engagement. She would like your input on the decorations in your new bedchamber."

She turned her eyes to his as a new desire hovered below the surface at his mention of their living arrangements. He saw it too and caught her lips. passion seeping into the touch. He pulled back, and she breathlessly stepped out of his reach.

"On second thought, I think it an excellent thing that I won't see you again until our wedding day."

Peter laughed, catching her again and placing another lasting kiss to her lips.

Peter was right. She did not notice the week passing. Besides meeting formally with Peter's mother, she orchestrated her packing. She did not think she would finish in time. Though it would not matter in the end. She would be so close. She could come after the festivities to complete her task.

The day of her wedding arrived, and everything was

in place. She moved down the stairs in her new gown, made specially for the day, a luxury, she knew. Sarah had placed flowers in her hair before handing her a cluster of roses, peonies, and herbs from the garden, all tied together with love knots made from ribbons. She caught her father's adoring smile before catching sight of Peter. Her breath hitched, seeing him dressed to the nines, more put together than she had ever seen him before. Peter took her arm as she stepped onto the tile with her silk-stocking slippers.

"You are perfect," he whispered.

"Are you ready for the walk to the church, Father?"

Her father just smiled as Peter led her out the front entrance of her home. She looked to Peter and then to the new carriage waiting in front.

"It is your first wedding present."

"You are giving me too much," she breathed.

"Nothing is too much for you, my dear Juliana." He handed her into the open carriage, followed by her father.

The drive was short, and they were greeted by what seemed like half the townspeople standing in the churchyard. She looked for Patience to no avail. She knew it would have taken a miracle to get her here, given their last parting, but Juliana still hoped she would respond to the letter she sent, inviting her. She did not have long to ponder as Peter helped her from the carriage, giving her arm to her father before disappearing into the church.

Her aunt and uncle were waiting when they entered, along with Peter's mother and a man she had never seen before. Her father gave her to Peter as they stood in front of the vicar.

The ceremony was brief, and before she knew it, she was being ushered into the vestry. After all interested parties signed, the vicar reverently handed her a copy of the lines. She took in her breath at this formality. For one of her class, it was just a symbol. No one would question her marriage to Peter, but it was something she would cherish forever. She was officially Lady Berkshire. Now it seemed silly, caring so much for society's censure. The only people who truly mattered were the people here, those who came to wish them well. Her community, her family.

She looked again at her new ring. It was brilliant with small diamonds encased below the gold. But this was a little thing as she looked back to Peter. He smiled on her as he guided her out of the church, the bells ringing as their neighbors cheered their well wishes.

They were off in their new carriage, looks of envy coming from a few faces. She did not have the inclination to care, so happy she was to be Peter's wife.

CHAPTER 20

"WE ARE NOT LEAVING straightaway on our wedding trip?" Juliana looked concerned as they drove out of the churchyard, leaving everyone behind them.

Peter smiled lovingly. He could not believe this day had finally come. Juliana was well and truly his, and he would never lose her again. "No. I promised your father I would not take you off until after the breakfast."

"I think he has you wrapped around his finger already." She smiled, leaning into him as she wove her arm through his.

"I cannot resist something I know will bring you happiness." As he brought her closer, he felt as if she always belonged here, nestled in the crook of his neck with his arm safely around her.

"We will take a slight deviation from our plans though."

She looked at her surroundings before turning her eyes to his. "Your home?" An adorable questioning look marred her features. It was better than any of the angry fiery contempts she had so often given him in their youth.

"Our home," he corrected.

When the carriage came to a stop, Peter helped her out. His driver knew what to do, but Juliana turned surprised eyes to him as it left the drive, leaving them alone. She followed him into the house, darting her eyes to the waiting maid, then back to him. She gulped before turning a delightful shade of pink, one that matched the flowers in her wedding bouquet.

"She will show you to your room." Peter gestured to the maid.

Juliana's eyes widened. "Peter, this is scandalous even for you. It is still morning!"

Peter threw his head back with a laugh. He could not help teasing Juliana, but he didn't intend for her to come up with the idea that had floated through his mind at being alone with her for the first time as husband and wife. And he never intended to act upon the idea. He pulled her to him, kissing her nose.

"I have left a present for you on your bed. Change quickly and meet me on the landing. I will not move from this spot, my love."

She pulled herself from his embrace and scurried up the stairs. He wished he could see her reaction to her newly decorated room but knew that would be too much a temptation for him.

She was next to him before he could think more fully on the matter, her eyes shining. She knew exactly where he intended to take her just by his second present. She was too clever for her own good.

"I could have produced my walking boots, you know. Ones that matched my dress better. I am going to need to change again once we reach my father's house."

"I have many surprises for you this day. Come." He tugged her out the door, and they walked hand-in-hand up the path to the lake.

The walk was short, and as they picked their way up the slope, he heard something rustle in the water. Juliana glanced up, peering between the trees.

"Is someone there already?"

"There shouldn't be." Peter hoped no one was. It would interrupt his surprise.

With a grin, Juliana made her way up the slope until she stood at the edge of the lake, right next to the dock. Peter moved quickly behind her. A flock of ducks splashed in the water. The family looked as they always had every year, flopping around and poking each other. The ducks noticed them watching and stopped their playing and glided over to the bank. Juliana had trained them well. He had to admit to himself that she had a strong claim to the lake because these ducks knew her. He moved to the bank and pushed a small rowboat into the water, tying it to the small makeshift dock.

"I missed this lake."

"I think the lake missed you, too. And so did your little feathered friends." The ducks swam away as he jumped off the dock, reaching her side again. Peter grinned, taking her hand. "I had this boat built for you. Would you like to try it out?"

She looked skeptically toward it, then to her new dress, and finally his finery. "I'm happy to see it is nothing like the rowboat I painted in London."

Peter laughed and guided her onto the dock, jumping into the boat, making it rock on the still water. He reached for her hand, and she stepped down, shaking awkwardly when the boat tilted.

"We'll capsize!" she laughed as she collapsed into her seat.

"Nonsense. It is safe." He untied the boat and took up the oars, pulling them further into the lake.

Juliana breathed in the warm air, absorbing the beauty of their surroundings. "Your mother captured this lake in a way I never could."

He saw a sudden excitement blossom in her. "What are you thinking?"

"Your mother is now my mother. Perhaps she can teach me how to paint, now that we are so intimately acquainted."

Peter rested back, eyeing her with a smile. "She is in

much better spirits than when I left her. It is because of you."

"What have I done?"

"She has been waiting for my marriage, even though I am not old enough for her to be concerned. She always loved you. You were not just a sister I never had. You were also a daughter to her in a way."

"I thought you no longer think of me as a sister."

He shook his head at her grin. "Believe me when I tell you that you hold a much higher regard in my heart."

That seemed to please her as her smile broadened. She looked at the ducks now following them, and her smile fell. "I wonder why Patience did not come to the wedding. I sent her an invitation."

"I'm not sure how willing her parents were to face us again."

Juliana cast her gaze out to the lake she loved so well. "I feel that Patience's new situation was all my doing."

Peter reached for her hand, squeezing it. "Do not blame yourself, Juliana. You couldn't have known the outcome."

"I feel guilty all the same. I will need to see Patience again before I can gain any kind of closure."

Peter nodded, releasing her hand and setting back to rowing. "I am sorry," he said after a long silence. "In that moment when her parents told her they were taking her away to the country—I should have said something. But they were already so angry at me. I feared making things worse."

"You did the right thing. Nothing you said could have changed their minds."

Peter nodded solemnly, wondering how the conversation had turned so quickly. "Wounds will heal." He fixed his gaze on Juliana. "I count ourselves lucky. Who knew the rambunctious girl of my youth would one day be my wife?"

Juliana gave him a smirk. "Who knew the conceited boy who always made time to tease me would become my handsome husband?"

Peter tilted his head. "You thought I was conceited?"

Juliana laughed. "Yes! You bragged, showed off your archery skills whenever I was around and constantly told me to act my age."

"It sounds like I was in love with you even then." He paused his rowing and reached out, stroking her chin with his thumb. She leaned into his touch, and he relished the way she looked at him.

"Perhaps you were," she breathed.

He leaned forward, parting the distance between them. He pressed his lips against hers. When she closed her eyes, she hummed in pleasure. They broke away, and he smiled at her breathless state, though it caused his pulse to quicken. He pushed down thoughts of her to tell her his biggest surprise yet.

"Are you ready for your next wedding gift?"

"You are not done yet?"

"I will never be done."

"I had no idea you were such a romantic." Her smile told him she was happy of the fact.

He cleared his throat, trying to concentrate on his objective. He had thought being alone with her before their marriage was hard, but that was nothing compared to this new pull they shared. "Our wedding trip."

"Yes," she coaxed when he paused.

He hoped he was doing the right thing. He might get her hopes up for nothing if Patience's parents refused them an audience.

"We will travel to the ocean."

Her eyes widened as her smile stretched.

"There is more. I have arranged to stop in Wallingford and visit Patience on the way."

Juliana squealed. "Truly!"

"Yes, but do not get your hopes up. I have arranged a stay at the inn near their home but have not talked to her parents. I do not know how they will react to us visiting unannounced."

She clapped her hands, unable to contain her excitement. "I am sure it will turn out well!"

Peter chuckled as he pulled the boat back to the dock, jumping out and tying it up. It was time to join their party. They would be missed if they didn't appear soon. He held his hand to Juliana, helping her from the boat. When she was safely on firm ground, she cast her gaze over the lake as it glittered under the rising sun. "I suppose this really is your lake now that we're married." Peter laughed, taking her hand. "Why are you so intent on insisting this lake is your property?"

Juliana looked over the lake. "It was one of the few memories I have of my mother. She would bring me here, just the two of us. I remember toddling down the slope, my mother holding my hand firmly so I would not fall. I always pictured bringing my children to this lake, just as she did, to feed the ducks by its edge. A new happy memory for me to treasure."

Peter caressed her cheek before turning and pulling her toward her new home. She dug her heels into the soft ground, and he turned back to her with a smile. "What is it, my love?"

She looked heavenward, and he had to work hard at not taking her into his arms and kissing the irritation from her lips.

"The wedding breakfast is the other way!"

He just smiled before pulling her back down the slope.

"Peter," she scolded. "What is in that head of yours?"

He stopped, turning to her again.

"You are getting better than you think at painting pictures, for the image stuck in my head of our children playing by your side by our lake. I thought we should start right away in making that canvas a reality." He smiled mischievously at her before guiding her down further, wrapping his arm around her waist so she could not fall.

She looked to him, this time doing a terrible job of hiding her smile. "Peter, you know we have promised my father to be there in time for the cake."

He sighed dramatically before turning them toward her father's home. "If you insist. I must get used to my demanding wife."

Juliana giggled. "You are still such a boy."

He gave her a smile. "And I always will be." He placed a kiss to her cheek as he stopped, gazing at the lake. "It is our lake now. I intended to give it to you as another wedding present."

"No, Peter, you cannot take that pleasure. I intended it to be *your* wedding gift."

He silenced her with a kiss. They would have to practice this often. No more arguing over a silly lake. They had much better things to do now that they were a married couple, and he would enjoy it very much.

She pulled back, suddenly laughing.

"What?"

"I was thinking of candle wax. Do you think we'll ever know?"

"I'm thinking Lord Danbury counts his riches by candle light." Peter covered her lips with a kiss.

EPILOGUE

PATIENCE STEELED herself as she moved through the garden deep into the hedges before she settled on a stone beach. Looking both ways, careful before extracting the letter from her apron pocket.

The old butler had secreted the letter before her mother had seen it, or she would have never known her friend, Juliana, had written.

She broke the seal eagerly and read. Her heart did somersaults rejoicing in knowing Walter had not written the letter that sent her and Juliana into danger. A fact her parents had no knowledge of. It was bad enough to return home to the country in disgrace. Had her parents known of her escapades with Juliana, she'd be banished from London forever.

Her eyes widened, her hand gripping her chest. Could it be that Lady Allen was so devious as to send

Patience to certain ruin? Was it so important that Rebecca marry wealth or a title? Patience suspected it was for Lady Allen's benefit, not Rebecca's. She couldn't believe Lady Allen had sent her the letter. But here it was. Peter had confronted her at Juliana's ball.

She wished she'd been there. She wondered if Walter had heard. Surely it was in the gossip sheets.

She folded the letter and tucked it safely in her pocket. Standing, she reached for her basket and walked through the garden, checking the pedals on the rosebuds. She was careful to cut the stems the proper length. The length which her mother demanded.

Yes, her mother demanded many things, but she wasn't cruel. Not like Lady Allen. Patience could almost feel sorry for Rebecca who would not be able to show her face in London. Not for a while at least. Until some other scandal erupted.

Did Walter think her cruel? She would never give up hope, until Walter faced her and declared he no longer loved her.

Patience left the roses on the table in the kitchen and retreated to her room where she took a seat at her desk. Drawing a fresh piece of paper, she picked up her pen. Hesitation hung as she bit her bottom lip. She carefully penned, "My dear Walter…"

She scribbled another two sentences, then crossed them out, frustrated. What more could she say that hadn't been said in her last letter to him just before leaving London? She'd explained her side of the story—that she did not love Lord Berkshire and never had. That he loved her friend Juliana. Perhaps she could write Walter and tell him of the impending wedding.

Her hand hovered over the blank parchment, a dollop of ink hanging from the tip of her pen.

If he hadn't responded to her first letter, would he care at all about Lord Berkshire and Juliana? Would he care about her?

She blotted the ink before she wrote, "I am trapped in a cage of suppressed emotion and unrequited love."

It was a bit dramatic and not like her at all.

She stared bitterly at her words before crumpling the paper and giving up, tossing the wad across the room. It was useless writing Walter another letter she doubted he would respond.

A knock sounded on her door.

"Patience, come to dinner at once."

Her brow creased as her mother moved away, foot falls echoing down the hall. She knew why a servant hadn't been sent to fetch her. Her mother wanted to wield her control. Let Patience know she would not be ignored. As melodramatic as it seemed, Patience wanted to stay locked in her room, pining after a man she could not have while silently rebelling against her mother's iron fist.

She didn't care if she starved.

But she was a coward like her father, not daring to

cross her mother. She made her way reluctantly down the stairs and into the dining room. Her parents, already seated, not bothering to wait as a servant set food in front of them. Patience took her seat at the left of her father, across from her mother, refusing to look at them. She sat in silence, not bothering to make conversation. It didn't matter, her father was reading the paper, her mother buttering her bread.

"Oh," her father's startled outburst, stopped both women, their eyes turned to him. It was a rare occurrence to have her father make any sounds over dinner.

"Well. What is it?" her mother asked testily when it became apparent that her father was not going to enlighten them on his own.

Her father squinted, continuing his reading, not bothering to acknowledge her mother's annoyed tone. He cleared his throat, not looking at either of them.

"Daniel Longman has passed away," he breathed, a troubled expression on his brow.

Patience's stomach lurched, upsetting the food that had settled there.

"Walter's brother?" she whispered.

"How did he die?" Her mother seemed interested.

Patience, though most likely for different reasons. Her mother always had to be in the know about everyone so she could be the first to spread the best bits of gossip throughout the neighborhood.

"Carriage accident, it seems." He lifted his head from the paper.

Patience exchanged a glance with her mother. Was that distress she saw?

"A carriage accident? How?" Her mother's voice broke.

"It's vague," Her father shrugged. Folding the newspaper, he set it beside his plate.

Patience snatched it up before her mother could say any more on the subject. She flipped through the pages, finding the story and reading over as she discovered the details for herself.

"Poor Walter," she murmured.

Her father tore a chunk of bread with his fingers.

"He's set to inherit his family's estate now that his brother has passed." he mumbled to himself.

Patience's eyes widened. She swallowed as her mind raced. Walter would be heartbroken.

Her mother's eyes drilled into her father's. "Unlikely he'll claim it. He's too busy becoming a barrister in London."

"He must return home to sort out the family affairs. He has his younger sister to look after." His eyes grew distant. "As well as his mother. He wouldn't abandon them." He shook his head, as if coming out of a fog.

Her father's words replayed in her head. He'll need to return home. Walter would return to Wallingford if only for a little while to set his affairs in order. He now had the estate to look after. Not as wealthy as Lord Berkshire's but enough to settle down — Patience's eyes returned to her mother.

THANKS FOR READING Peter and Juliana's story.

To find out what happens to Patience and Walter, click HERE. On Amazon.

Reviews are welcome and appreciated!

ABOUT THE AUTHOR

As Karen Lynne, I write sweet historical romances, regency period being my favorite.

I love history and have been reading hundreds of romances since high school. Timeless authors where the hero and heroine are virtuous with sweet happy endings.

When I am not writing, I enjoy time with my sweetheart, my children and grandchildren and long lunches with my two reading buddies. You know who you are.

Gardening vegetables and fruits in my garden and living in our 1863 stone cottage in the Rocky Mountains.

Life is good!

Printed in Great Britain
by Amazon